CREEPY CAMPFIRE TALES

Halloween Camp Out

Enjoy the campfires!

James D Adams

CREEPY CAMPFIRE TALES

Halloween Camp Out

James D. Adams

Owl Creek Media Ltd

Jasper, Ohio

OWL CREEK MEDIA Ltd.

P.O. BOX 235

Jasper, Ohio 45642

www.owlcreekmedia.com

Designed & Edited by
James H. Dennewitz III

Back Cover Photo
Kathy McQuay

10 9 8 7 6 5 4 3 2 1

Library of Congress
Cataloging-in-Publication Data
Adams, James D., 1967-
Creepy campfire tales Hallowwen Camp
Out James D. Adams
CIP

ISBN
978-1-60404-103-3

Proudly Printed in the U.S.A.

For my wife, Kimberly, who types all my writing projects into the computer and never complains about my sloppy handwriting. She has stuck with me through much scarier situations than those found in this book and has always believed in my dreams and listened to my nightmares.

Other Books by James D. Adams

Hopper's Pond - The Symphony Of Life
ISBN: 978-1-60404-100-2

Rockwell, New Hampshire Series -
Coming Summer 2008
ISBN: 978-1-60404-603-8

Dark Valley Ohio Series - The Fright Festival
Coming September, 2008
ISBN: 978-1-60404-113-2

FrankenEinstein Series
Coming Fall 2008
ISBN: 978-1-60404-145-5

Phantom Hall Series
Coming October, 2008
ISBN: 978-1-60404-132-3

Dark Valley Ohio Series - Slasher's Mansion
Coming Fall 2009
ISBN: 978-1-60404-114-9

Creepy Campfire Tales Vol. 2 - Halloween Party
Coming Fall 2009
ISBN: 978-1-60404-105-6

Author Web Site
www.JamesDAdams.com

Contents

In memory of Harold Dean Evans
I shared more campfires and ghost stories
with Dean than anyone else over the years.
His friendship was a warm, steady part of
my life that vanished too soon.
He is missed beyond words.

Introduction

Campfires have been a part of human history for untold thousands of years. I suspect our early ancestors also told scary stories around those first fires, so it's not surprising that bon fires played a central role in the first Samhain, which we now call Halloween. There's just something creepy about watching the flames consume in a matter of hours something that took centuries to grow. It's a reminder to us all how precious and fragile life can be. It was this thought and this fear that Halloween sprung up around, combined with Autumn being the time to bring in the harvest, a time when the fruits of mankind's labor could be enjoyed for a brief spell. But death shrouded winter lurked just beyond the warmth of the Halloween bon fires, so our ancestors told creepy tales and did their best to avoid any ghosts that might be prowling about on Halloween Night. Any evil associated with this night is not ancient, but a modern perversion of the true spirit of Halloween, which is a celebration of the harvest and a rehearsal for our deaths. But in the spirit of sharing scary tales around a fire at October's end, the stories that made it into the book take place in the fall. As for the stories that didn't make it into this book, well, I used them to start a campfire.

1

CREEPY'S WARNING

There is something special about October wind that brings me to life each Halloween season. Maybe it's the scent of death, picked up by dieing and decaying leaves and rotting weeds, or perhaps the dust of floating golden rod mingled with lifeless, dried out corn stalks forms an evil potion that causes the dead to rise and ghosts to stir.

Whatever causes this phenomenon, this same October wind has the nasty habit of bringing forth monsters from the Nether Regions. A night of telling creepy campfire tales would not be completely creepy without some mention of a few of these monsters.

Now, pull up your jacket collar to protect your neck, slide next to someone, and move closer to the fire because your blood's about to run cold. But if we stir up something evil from beyond the trees, your blood may soon be dead cold.

If a sudden breeze makes you shiver, or shadows crawl like spiders across your face; if something moves behind you, it's probably just the wind, but it could be something creepy.

Scarecrow Dance

Smoke from dozens of campfires drifted and swirled in the early October breeze that shook brilliant red and yellow leaves loose from the trees of New Hampshire State Park. Wind swirled with the drone of conversations and crackling campfires, preventing any campers from hearing the approaching footsteps from within the dark woods.

The burning embers of the campfires cast an eerie, swaying glow against motor homes, pop up campers, and tents. Wood ash, smoke and moist pine needles mixed with the scent of dried leaves and damp ground.

Sam Watkins sat roasting a hot dog,

remembering the fun days of summer vacation and looking forward to his 13th and final Trick or Treat.

"Did you make any new friends today?" his mom asked from across the fire ring.

"Just one, a kid named Brad from Concord. He wants to be a magician."

"That sounds fun," his dad answered. "Though not too many make a living at that."

He shrugged off the comment as the heat from the fire warmed his face in spite of the nip in the air. He looked across the heat rising from the orange flames at his mom and dad sipping on their hot chocolate, feeling glad they took him camping, even if nothing exciting ever happened. Sam had no reason to believe this campout would be an exception.

"Brad said he'd stop by before they pulled out tomorrow," Sam said as he removed his hot dog from the flame and slid it off the stick into a bun.

"We're pulling out early this time. You're mom wants to go out the back way and drive over to Annie's Orchard, then have lunch in Walpole. I hear there's some nice farm country that way," his dad said.

"Maybe I'll go by his site then," Sam said. "We are gonna try to meet up at the Pumpkin Festival in Keene."

"What was that?" his mom asked and bolted up to her feet, staring into the woods.

"I don't know, but it sounded big," Sam said, then took a bite of his hot dog.

"Probably just a deer," his dad said.

"There it is again," his mom said. "Maybe we should get inside the camper."

"Sounded like more than one this time," Sam said while chewing.

"That's no deer. It could be a bear," his mom said.

"Maybe we'd better step inside," Sam's dad agreed.

Before they could take a step, the autumn air exploded with scarecrows flipping and flopping their arms, kicking up their legs and shaking their heads.

"You scared us to death," Sam's mom said, then smiled sheepishly.

Sam laughed. "Awesome!"

"I didn't know there would be entertainers tonight. The Halloween campout's not for another 2 weeks," his dad said.

The scarecrows didn't reply, they just kept dancing. One in a dusty old brown farm coat and tall hat grabbed his mom's hands and swung her in circles. Another scarecrow in pin striped bibs and a red flannel shirt jumped up onto the picnic table, kicking off the radio and the Peterboro basket, sending napkins and paper plates flying into a pile of leaves. As the scarecrow suddenly released her, another smashed a pumpkin against the side of their camper.

"Hey now. You just cost yourselves a

job," his father said as he knelt down to help up his mom. "When I tell the park ranger about this -"

Before he could finish, another scarecrow dumped a bag of trash on his father, who then rose up swinging his fists at the scarecrows. They flopped their arms wildly, smacking his dad repeatedly. Another one started pelting the camp with ears of corn.

Sam ran towards the one in the brown barn coat, but it jumped into the air just as Sam leapt to tackle him, sending him into face first into a pile of leaves.

He turned around and looked up to see five of the scarecrows running away toward other campsites. The one in the pin stripe bibs and flannel shirt jumped up onto the top of their camper and stomped madly as he cackled ferociously while clangs and thuds rang out from inside. Sam's dad stood on the cooler and reached up for the scarecrow's legs, but it jumped over and then around them. The scarecrow pulled some straw out from under it's flannel shirt and threw it in his dad's face, then it leapt to the ground and hobbled across the road to terrorize the next campsite.

"I'm going to get the ranger. You two better get inside until I get back," his dad said and took off for the office.

Sam and his mom hurried up the metal steps and into the camper. His mom snapped the lock behind them.

"I'm going to wash off. Stay inside until

your father returns," his mom said as she picked up dishes from the floor and placed them in the kitchenette sink. "Those jerks messed with the wrong people," she said and slammed the overhead cabinet doors before sliding into the tiny bathroom.

"I can't believe that guy jumped up on the roof like that," Sam said as he sat down on his knees on the narrow seat and peeked through a small gap in the curtains. He heard a woman scream and a man swearing in machine gun fashion. Several people ran, clutching an armful of belongings. Ears of corn and pumpkins lie scattered on the road. Pumpkin guts clung to the sides of several maples. He saw two of the scarecrows dancing around a fire as they threw radios and lanterns and food into the flames. Then the scarecrow with the old brown barn coat ran by dragging a tent full of screaming people behind him. The tent bulged and rose as they struggled to find a way out. Sam slid the window open and yelled through the screen, "Stop it you jerk! You're hurting them!"

The scarecrow stopped, looked at Sam and starting dancing on top of the tent.

"Stop it!" he yelled. Smack. A scarecrow face popped up against his on the other side of the screen and Sam shot backwards and twisted his ankle as he fell into the stairwell by the door. Then a screechy voice filled the camper.

"You people are all the same. You hang

scarecrows outside to rot in the heat and the rain, while you hunker down under cozy little roofs. But when we realized you were also going to leave us out in the cold -"

Another scarecrow head suddenly popped up, dust flying out of the burlap that formed his head as he spoke, "That was the last straw!" They laughed, then a moment later a huge pumpkin landed and smashed on their windshield.

A woman from the tent emerged, "You're a creep!"

The tall scarecrow in the brown barn coat turned and said, "Actually ma'am my name's Creepy. That's C, R, double E, single P, Y." He blew a huge brown cloud of dust and hay particles in her face, then cackled like a witch. "Come on boys; let's waltz right out of here and back into the October night."

The other scarecrows soon emerged and followed Creepy back into the forest, singing a haunting tune:

"Creepy Campfire Tales, Something Creepy's going on,
When midnight comes, the campers scream and run,
And in the morning, they will be dead and gone.
Ghouls And Goblins crawl out of graves, scarecrows dance across hay bales,
Searching for dark campsites,
Creepy Campfire Tales."

"I can't believe no one was seriously injured last night," Sam's dad said as they pulled out of the campground the next morning.

"Tell that to my ankle," Sam said. "It's still pretty sore."

His mom turned her head to look at him on the little couch. "Those idiots could have killed somebody, so I think we came out pretty lucky."

And so the conversation went until a mile or so later they came upon an endless field of corn. Every hundred feet or so along the edge of the field, hung a different weathered scarecrow. His mother looked away. "I don't ever want to see another scarecrow again. I hope they catch the men that did that."

Sam realized no man would ever face punishment for what had happened as they passed a scarecrow in striped bibs and a flannel shirt. A cold shiver shot through his body as he began to wrap his mind around the fact that what had visited their campground were not men dressed as scarecrows, but actual scarecrows that now hung from their poles, guarding the corn.

He slipped on his LL Bean coat to warm himself as they drove past a scarecrow in a dusty, old, brown barn coat and a tall hat. He began to sway slowly, fear squeezing his throat as he whispered, "That one's name is Creepy. That's C, R, double E, single P, Y.

Halloween Hayride

The ranger yelled "All aboard," to the line of people waiting to take the first ever Halloween hayride at the Ben Franklin Campground in New Hampshire.

"I can't believe our parents actually let us go," Meagan said. "Eight years of friendship and this is like the first thing we've gotten to do together without them."

"Wave at my mom. She's over on the porch of the General Store waving wildly as we board," Brenna said.

They stepped up onto the hay wagon and sat down on a bale of straw, then turned and waved vigorously at Brenna's mom, both of them smiling. "She still thinks I'm twelve," Brenna said from the corner of her mouth.

"So does my mom. Dad thinks I'm nine." Meagan stopped waving, then turned to face the front of the hay wagon and the back of the tractor. Brenna pulled out a quilt from her canvas bag and Meagan grabbed one corner and pulled it over them. The tractor lurched forward into the deepening darkness of late twilight, belching black diesel smoke back at them. They eased through the parking lot, then past the waste station and dumpsters, and finally left the pavement and entered the thick woods. Maple trees full of orange and yellow leaves formed a tunnel above their heads and White Birch trees shone in the headlights of the tractor like ghosts twisting up into the sky. The wagon creaked and moaned as the uneven ground below made it rock and sway. The noises of the campground faded and the steady clanking of the tractor engine, twisting of the wagon boards, and swishing straw became the only noticeable sounds. A breeze cold as the grave slithered around them. Then, from the depths of the woods, rose a high pitch waling.

"Was that a wolf?" Brenna asked the other people on the wagon.

A lady near the front spoke up. "It might have been coyotes, but it wasn't a wolf."

A man across the aisle from them spoke, "I've been roaming these woods my whole life and I've never heard anything like that before."

"There it is again," Meagan said. She inched closer to Brenna and away from the edge of the hay wagon.

"Do you suppose he can hear that over the sound of the tractor?" Brenna asked while looking at the back of the driver's head.

"My friends warned us about coming to this campground," a blonde girl said. "My parents said all Jr. High kids try to scare their friends around Halloween time, but I knew my friends were serious."

Brenna looked alarmed. "What did they say?"

The man across from them cut in, "Now girls, don't go scaring yourselves with a bunch of creepy campfire tales." He smiled at the blonde girl scanning the depths of the woods intently. "Your friends may have been serious, but they were probably just repeating urban legends."

The girl looked at him earnestly. "These weren't legends. My friend Kayla said her grandpa told her he had gone hunting in these woods as a boy once – only once."

"What did he see?" Meagan asked. "Were there wolves?"

"Let her finish," Brenna prodded.

"He said they saw creatures with big teeth and weird ears and that his uncle died saving him from the monsters. I've heard other people say this forest is cursed, that's why I came. I want to show everyone

15

back at school I'm not afraid of the big, bad wolf."

The man laughed, but by now, all twelve people on the wagon were watching and listening to the blonde girl. "I think your friend's grandpa was just having a little fun with her."

Thump. Everyone, including the man, jumped as something hit the bottom of the wagon.

"It's under the wagon!" the blonde girl screamed.

"What is it?" Brenna pleaded as she clutched Meagan tightly.

The man looked worried, but he spoke calmly. "We probably hit a small animal of some sort."

A flurry of autumn leaves shook loose from the trees overhead and fell onto the wagon.

Meagan pulled her arm out from under the quilt and pointed up into the trees. "There's something up there."

Everyone on the wagon looked up and saw movement somewhere: A long arm with claws in an Oak tree, red eyes in a Maple, pointy ears in a Birch, a series of quick jumps and leaps in several other trees, but no one ever clearly saw an entire creature. Panic tore through the wagon and everyone screamed at the driver to speed up.

A flash of red light from the brake lights washed across their faces as the driver brought the wagon to a stop and turned partially around in his seat to look back at the passengers. Initially he was smiling, obviously expecting some Halloween shenanigans, but his face grew grim as he surveyed the looks of genuine horror on everyone's faces as they shouted different pleas at the same time. "Go! Don't stop! Hurry! Get going!"

Another high-pitched wailing ripped through the cool autumn air. Several creatures sprang from the woods, vaguely visible in the red tail light glow. They opened their mouths and displayed glimpses of long, pointy teeth. The driver's eyes grew wide when he saw the shadowed creatures approaching the wagon. He spun back around and shoved the tractor into fourth gear this time, grinding the gears as he did. "Hold on, top speed is only sixteen miles an hour, but it's fast enough to shake you off the wagon. I only hope it's fast enough to outrun them."

The creatures looked less then four feet tall, but at least a dozen more of them emerged from the woods to chase the wagon full of frantic people. One jumped onto the side of the tractor and the driver kicked it off.

Another thump rattled the floorboards of the wagon as they took off down the dirt path. One of the things jumped onto a bale of straw, another one grabbed hold of the railing on the back of the wagon and everyone screamed again. The driver didn't turn around this time. Loose straw spun in circles and flew through the air at blinding speed. One by one, the other creatures began to lose the chase.

The man slid across the straw, struggling to stay on as the wagon picked up speed. He shoved the first creature off the bale of straw and sent it tumbling off the side of the wagon. Then the thing under them shook loose as the tractor hit top speed. The man fell onto Brenna and Meagan then rolled onto the floor, striking his head. He grabbed his head, and his eyes started closing.

"Brenna, it's climbing over the railing!" Meagan shouted.

Brenna and Meagan both stood, keeping their knees slightly bent and holding onto each other as the wagon swayed from side to side and rose and fell in quick bursts as the tires ran over the bumpy, granite covered ground of the woods. Brenna looked over the edge just as two bales of straw flew off the wagon and bounced, then split in two as it knocked down the last creature still keeping pace with the wagon. Sixteen mph was dangerously fast on a hay wagon tearing through a forest with low hanging branches.

"Grab that end," Brenna said as she fell forward onto a bale of straw.

They picked up the straw by the binder twine and lifted it into the air as the creature climbed to the top of the back rail. The

straw struck it in the face and the creature grabbed hold of the bale. In the same
instance, the girls let go of the bale and it,
along with the creature, fell from the back
of the wagon as Brenna and Meagan both
fell into a small pile of some of the remaining straw.

They lay there in disbelief, watching
the tree limbs speed by for several minutes
until stars replaced them as they left the
woods, slowed down, and pulled back into
the campground.

Brenna couldn't sleep that night. She
was too angry and too scared. Their canvas top pop up camper wasn't much protec-
tion if those monsters came up out of the
woods to the camping area. She couldn't
believe her parents had written off their
horrible story as a Halloween prank. The
tractor driver had taken off as soon as
they unloaded, but not before he assured
those waiting for the wagon's return that
some local kids had scared everyone on the
hayride. The more the wagon riders pro-
tested his story, the more the waiting crowd
laughed. A few looked uncertain, but didn't
want to go against the majority. The driver
said the tractor was losing engine pressure
and there'd be no more hayrides. Most people were too mad about waiting for nothing
to consider they may be in danger.

But the ranger knew they weren't' kids
in costumes so why hadn't he evacuated
the campground? Did he think they'd form

a hunting squad and kill all the creatures before word got out and their business was ruined?

Brenna stared at the ceiling of her camper, praying for Sunday morning to arrive so they could pack up and go home. But if those things weren't afraid of tents and campers – she shook the nightmare images of their long, sharp teeth from her mind. She glanced over at the glowing Big Ben clock: 2:30 am. Most of the campfires would be out or burned down to embers by now. She didn't really smell smoke anymore. What if the fires had kept them away? They were mostly out now. She pulled the covers up over her head, but they didn't drown out the sound of a high pitch howling that tore through her spine from the nearby woods.

Frozen with fear, she called out to her parents, but they didn't respond. Hundreds of piercing howls from every direction drowned out her voice.

Then she heard the screaming.

Campfire Stranger

Gene tossed two logs onto the camp-fire and sparks shot up into the sky. Red flames twisted and stretched when another blast of chilly autumn wind slith-ered across the maple trees, shaking loose a shower of colored leaves.

"That should warm up you love birds," Gene said to Lisa who was sitting on Mike's lap.

"We're not love birds, we're soul mates," Lisa said.

"Ignore him," Stacey said as she clung to Stan's arm. "All that hot chocolate has made him annoying."

"You shouldn't blame it on the hot choc-olate," Mike said and they laughed.

21

"You guys are all whacked. There's no such thing as a soul anyway," Gene said and sat down.

"You're wrong about that. I can assure you," a low rumbling voice from the woods said. A haggard man appeared in the glow of their campsite and drifted over to the fire ring to warm his hands. "If you ever see a haunted soul, you'll know I'm right.

Everyone stood up and moved away from the midnight stranger. "My Mom and Dad are in our camper mister," Mike said. "If you have any funny ideas . . ."

The stranger curled up the left corner of his mouth, but not even a hint of amusement accompanied the gesture. "I can almost feel the heat of your fire. Just the sight of it is distantly comforting."

"Are you a camper here, because you look lost?" Gene said.

"What would someone his age be doing in the woods at night," Stan remarked.

"I have roamed forests and caverns and other dark secluded places for years now. Ever since my family was murdered, I have attempted to disengage from society."

"You poor man," Lisa said. "That must have been awful."

"Did they catch the guy?" Mike asked.

"They never caught anyone, not even when others in our town got killed," the stranger said.

"Figures," Stan said as he put his arm around Stacey. "Cops don't do so well with serial killers."

The man looked up at Stan. His gaze seemed to have captured the image of the campfire. "This wasn't a serial killer. Not like John Wayne Gacy at least. More like Ted Bundy."

"What's the difference?" Gene asked.

"John was a man who killed people. Ted was a man who was used by demons to kill people," the stranger said, then looked at each of them in turn. "Demons make some people kill. Evil, relentless demons."

Gene shook his head. "Souls and demons. My Dad says all that stuff's a bunch of crap, that evil men like to blame demons and devils instead of taking responsibility for what they did."

"Let him get this off his chest," Stan said.

"I believe in evil spirits," Lisa said. "I've read an awful lot of stories about people who were haunted by evil spirits."

"It all seems a little hard to believe to me," Mike said.

The man turned toward Mike, making a scar across his forehead visible. "Believe it. I was completely normal. I never harmed a fly my entire life, until we moved into that house."

Stan chuckled nervously, "What are you saying exactly?"

The stranger's face was a weave of fire-light and shadow and the flames reflected in his eyes. "I loved my family. I loved my neighbors. Then one foggy day, I met a man in the graveyard on our property. He told me he had been wandering for years, then he vanished into the fog. At that moment, I felt the urge to kill for the first time in my life. Just seeing another person made me want to kill them. To silence their life force."

Gene pulled out his pocketknife and opened it, "Are you telling us you killed your family you psycho?"

"No, of course not. It was the demon. The man in the graveyard had freed himself when he released the demon into me. Soon, after killing my family, the demon started talking to me, urging me to kill others. I finally got the strength to resist him, but by then I had killed over a dozen people."

The girls slid behind the boys, who were all backing away from the stranger now.

"Dad! Dad!" Mike yelled at their camper.

"Just keep your distance," Gene said.

The stranger smiled, but only evil emanated from his face. "Roam the woods, stay away from people; it will help reduce the killing. But 12 becomes 50, then 100, then 500." He looked at Gene. "Still, if you're like me, you'll hate to pass on this curse to someone else, but sooner or later, you just have to get away from all the bloody murders. Forgive me, but your belief in a soul is about to be restored."

Then a blast of wind stirred up a cloud of gray smoke and the stranger sailed off into the black sky with it.

"Oh my God, he just vanished," Mike said. "I can't believe it, the guy vanished."

The girls buried their heads in the chests of their boyfriends.

"That was terrifying," Stacey said.

"Where could he have gone?" Stan asked.

"I told you, Gene. I told you there are ghosts & evil spirits," Lisa said.

Then in a low, rumbling voice that sounded more demonic than human, Gene spoke. "I can assure you, I'm no evil spirit. I'm pure demon. It appears I already have a knife, how convenient. You have all been great friends over the years, but I think I see what the stranger meant about the urge to kill. It's unstoppable." Gene circled them like a wolf herding its prey. He smiled as his knife blade glistened in the flaring fire light. Gene opened his mouth, but did not move his lips, yet he spoke. "Let the slaughter begin."

Pumpkin Carving

Black clouds gathered over the Green Mountain Campground just as the Annual Halloween Camp out pumpkin carving contest began. Sixteen-year-old Lucy Stevens watched her little sister Kelsey from the front row of straw bales. Their mom sat next to Lucy, snapping picture after picture with the digital camera.

"Take your time Kelsey, you can do it," Lucy said.

Kelsey looked at her and grinned, then turned her back on the crowd along with the other twelve kids and sat down in front of her pumpkin.

A ranger walked out to the front center of the stage. "Our contestants will have five minutes to carve their best pumpkin. Then the judges will pick three winners. Let's hope the rain holds off."

As if on cue, thunder rumbled for the first time. The last remaining shadows fled as more dark clouds rolled over the campground. In the distance, Lucy could hear boaters revving up their engines, probably trying to reach the docks before the storm hit.

"This year's sponsor and judge is Damon Graves, a businessman who recently moved here from Dark Valley Ohio," the ranger said as she smiled at the tall man standing near the exit path. "Let's thank him for donating this year's pumpkins." The audience clapped.

Lucy barely heard his voice over the applause, but she thought his lips had said, 'Just passing through,' as he nodded in response to the crowd. Something in his eyes burned, but the flames looked cold. "That guy's creepy," Lucy whispered to her mom.

"You shouldn't judge people you don't know," her mom said, then resumed her photo shoot.

"Then why's he judging our contest?" Lucy said.

Her mother gave her the don't push it look.

"Ready pumpkin carvers, begin," the ranger shouted.

Little elbows darted forward and back

as pumpkin skin was sliced and removed. Tiny pumpkin flesh triangles and circles flopped to the floor as they carved the secret faces, keeping the crowd in suspense. Parents cheered and encouraged, blurring out each other so that only an occasional word became recognizable in the sea of cheering voices. Two more claps of thunder rolled across the camp before the contest ended, then the ranger blew her whistle from the front of the stage. "Now rotate your pumpkins and Mr. Graves will judge them."

Damon walked up onto the stage and reviewed each entry like a General inspecting his troops. He walked back to the edge of the stage. "They're all perfect – Just perfect Halloween creations. I'll let the ranger decide her favorites." He curled the edges of his lips up and revealed a slither of yellowed teeth before leaving the stage.

Lucy nudged her mom. "Anyone who would call that a smile is twisted."

The children on the stage slowly picked up their pumpkins and turned around. A collective gasp escaped from the crowd before the screaming and weeping began. Lucy's mom dropped the camera just before she fainted, but Lucy did not notice. She stared at what her ten-year-old sister held in her hand.

The pumpkins now contained the faces of the children, their facial expressions frozen in terror. As Lucy's eyes drifted up to where her sister's face should be, she saw orange pumpkin flesh with cut-out, triangular eyes and a nose, and a mouth full of square teeth. She looked at all the other kids and saw pumpkin flesh now covered their faces too. Then lightning flashed and all their new heads lit up yellow as if candles now flickered where their brains should be. The same color yellow of his smile. Lucy's body shivered, she felt frozen in place. The smell of vomit now drifted through the air as more and more people began to get sick. She turned to look at Damon Graves but saw only a fodder shock rustling in the wind.

Then her sister and the other kids on the stage lifted up off the stage and into the blackened sky and floated away into the storm.

Desperate to save their children, frantic parents reached toward the sky as rain burst forth from the dark clouds, but their hands only clutched cold October rain mixed with the slimy guts and seeds of carved pumpkins.

Dead Air

"I'll never forget the night I found a radio station playing the most haunting music I've ever heard," Lisa Cairns said. "The disc jockey acted insane and every guest was stranger than the one before. Then people started dieing."

John threw another log on the campfire to warm up the October night, and walked back to one of the wood benches that surrounded the large fire pit in his grandpa's woods. He kept his stomach sucked in just in case Lisa happened to look at him. She looked uncharacteristically serious, and Rich was already smirking. He hoped he wouldn't put her through the ringer as he did most people who told creepy campfire

31

tales.

"The disc jockey had a hollowness in his voice that made the most mundane comments sound downright sinister."

"Sounds like some weird pirate radio broadcast to me," Rich said, his voice echoing through the woods in the thin, late evening air.

"That's what I thought at first, until the guests started mentioning all the people they had murdered over the weekend and what great pleasure it had brought them. I still thought, or maybe hoped is a better word, that it was only a sick station full of people who had never dealt with the pain of losing someone they love." She sipped on her hot chocolate, collecting her thoughts. "The minor details of their conversation perplexed me. Some of them talked about street lamps filled with whale oil, brick streets, and names of places I had never heard of. I started to wonder if maybe these voices could be ghosts."

"Just because you hear some history buffs on the radio you think you have tuned into the Twilight Zone," Rich said.

Lisa reached into her brown flight jacket and pulled out a pack of apple chips. "It's hard to explain, but things plummeted into darker and darker territory the more I listened.

"Later that night, I heard the most horrible screams on that station. I still think those people were in agony. I can't tell you

why I believe this, it's just something I felt."
She opened the bag of chips and munched
one down. "You know as well as I do that
reality has special qualities that can't
always be described, only experienced. I've
seen lots of movies, and no matter how
many fake car crashes I see, none of them
compare to those sickening driver's ed.
films."

"When the screaming started, I put my
hands over my ears and hummed to myself
until I caught a glimpse of some happy
motorist buckling up," John said then took
a long drink of Hirsch's cider straight from
the jug.

"Wonder which ones felt more pain, the
ones screaming or the ones whimpering?"
Rich asked.

"That's a gruesome question," John
said.

"Those were the types of morbid
thoughts overtaking my mind the longer I
listened, yet I couldn't turn off the station.
Images of pleading people desperately trying
to escape beheadings, torture chambers,
and being burned alive at the stake filled
my mind with realistic clarity. I closed my
eyes to block out these nightmare visions.
It was like a movie playing right in front of
me. Nobody was safe from the indignities
inflicted by the crew, who seemed to delight
in the suffering they enacted. I wanted it to
end, but a voice, and I'm not sure if it was
coming from the radio or my mind, said the

carnage would never end. I felt hypnotized, and I couldn't snap out of the trance." She took another bite of apple chips and stirred a small pile of leaves with her foot. "I wasn't able to make myself turn it off, until they threatened me."

With the debarked fire stick, Rich pushed some smoldering logs into the middle of the flames to get them burning better. Hundreds of sparks floated into the tops of the maple tree branches hanging over the large fire pit. "What's this, a modern ghost story?"

"Let her tell it," John said as he stood up and walked over to get more wood by the cedar picnic table, giving Rich a frown as he passed in front of him.

Rich pulled off his Polaris ball cap and pushed back his thick brown hair, and then put his cap back on using both of his hands to position it just right. "Ah, but doubt is the first step toward belief. We only doubt what we'd rather not believe," Rich said.

"Save the philosophy for your memoirs. Go ahead, Lisa," John said as he carried two chunks of wood to the fire pit and threw them on top of the pile Rich had just formed. An autumn wind whipped and twisted the flames. He pulled out a slice of beef jerky from his tan L.L. Bean coat and tore off a bite as he walked behind Lisa and back to his seat.

"I find it hard to believe myself, but I know it happened. Exactly how, I'm still not

sure, but it scared me so bad I haven't listened to the radio since."

"Why did you think it was real and not
some big hoax?" John asked.

"It's hard to explain unless I start at the
beginning," Lisa said. "It was December, '04
and I was still living with my parents. I had
just finished the last of my exams earlier
that day, and two weeks of Christmas vacation stretched out ahead. I was tired from
all the cramming so I spent the evening in
my room until it was time for bed. I used
to like to go to sleep with music playing, so
I flipped on the radio. When I did, I heard
this weird, whining that sounded like than
an a.m. radio station, and sure enough, I
hadn't flipped the switch all the way up.
Just as I started to, I heard a voice say,
'Don't touch that dial. We have a special
guest tonight you don't want to miss. Yours
truly, Jack The Ripper.'" Lisa brushed back
her blonde hair as she stared into the fire.

"They had my interest at once. They
played this dark classical music piece and
I heard a woman screaming in the back-
ground. I opened up a bag of chips and
ended up eating the whole bag before I went
to bed." "What time had you started listening?" Rich asked and rubbed his hands
together over the fire.

"Sometime between twelve and one."

"Maybe we should turn on the radio in
a half an hour and see if we can pick up
this station," Rich said. "It may sound like

old folklore, but maybe you turned on the radio at exactly midnight on just the right wave band and you connected with something supernatural."

"You wouldn't like it if people made fun of your stories," John said.

"I'm being serious. All we have to do is tune in 105 and at midnight, we'll turn it on A.M. instead of F.M., then we'll know, is it live, or was it a nightmare."

"In spite of his wicked intentions," John started with a smile, "he may be onto something." He watched her for a moment as she considered this.

"I never thought of turning on the radio at a certain time, but I didn't want to hear that station again. The more I thought about it, the more I feared it. I stopped listening to the radio after that night."

Dark clouds slid across the moon and a shadow engulfed the woods. They sat quietly for a moment, the burning wood snapping in front of them and the wind stirring fallen leaves behind them. John couldn't believe Lisa was telling such a strange story. In all of their conversations at O.U.C., she had always seemed lighthearted and uninterested in anything paranormal. Of course, people usually do seem that way in the daylight. Darkness hid the world, but had a way of revealing secrets hidden in our souls.

"I kept telling myself to turn the station, but I felt absorbed by the music, hoping to hear anything that might reveal to me the truth about this broadcast. She rubbed her eyes, then looked at John. "The longer I listened, the more I feared for my life. You've had that feeling that someone's watching you, haven't you? This gave me the feeling that someone was listening to me."

"These sound like some morbid people," John said.

"Tell me about it." Lisa finished her drink and made momentary eye contact with Rich. "At one point, he said 'Someone is dying right now, can you guess who?' Then another guy, with a familiar voice answers, 'Is it Leroy Clemmons?' 'Leroy it is, in Dark Valley, Ohio. A man dressed in a scarecrow costume just slit him open with an old rusty hay rake. And this doesn't resemble anything used to rake dead, fallen leaves. Now, let's find out a little bit about our winner. So what's your name, ghoul friend?' the disc jockey asked and let out a round of wicked laughter. Maybe vengeful describes it better. When the winner answered Keith Langer, my heart tightened.

"He was a Waller deputy years ago," John said. "About a month before we moved away, he vanished."

"Did you know him?" Rich asked.

"Keith was my uncle, my mother's brother. I was a kid when he vanished, but I remember his voice, and that was definitely him. My mom said he was dead and no one ever found his body. But it was him. That's why the voice had sounded so familiar."

"Sounds like some sick late night show," Rich said.

"With really good impersonators, impersonating people who never became famous," John added as he gave Rich a shut up now look.

"I kept trying to think like Rich, but I had passed any possibility of comforting denial long before this," Lisa said as she gazed into the burning embers. "Any weirdo can get a show these days, so that week I drove to the phone company and looked through the yellow pages of about 40 different cities. I didn't find any 1313 broadcasting on our a.m. dial. I also called the paper in Dark Valley the next afternoon and they confirmed a murder of a boy named Russ "Leroy" Clemmons. The coroner listed the time of death as 1:13 a.m., about the same time I had been listening. I began to think someone at that station had a friend in the Sheriff's Department and had gotten an advance tip."

"Or they could have heard it on the scanner," Rich said.

"That's what I figured, until I read the article in the paper. It was after 10 a.m. that morning when his grandfather found the boy's body in the cornfield and notified the sheriff. All final doubts faded at that moment."

"Did they know any other things they shouldn't have?" John asked.

"Yeah, and some of them were about me. I did suspect some pirate radio show at first. As far as I knew at that moment, the Leroy Clemmons murder could have been pure fiction. Their list of guests seemed endless. Ted Bundy, Ed Gein, and the real Jack The Ripper, who claimed he had been no more than a modern day pimp trying to sway the bulk of business his way. He said the best way to compete was to eliminate the competition. Then they ran what they called a historic playback. I heard women screaming and moaning. I could hear the slicing of flesh, and the noises made me heave. Not only were they losing their lives, but every gruesome incision stripped away more of their humanity. I felt immersed in the violence like a helpless spectator. The most disturbing part of the broadcast came when everyone in the studio began laughing, making one sick joke after another. The more intense the violence, the more they enjoyed it." She zipped up her coat. "Real or imagined, there's nothing funny about someone's death."

"Why would anyone do that?" John said, shaking his head.

"That wasn't the worst of it." Lisa tossed the empty bag of apple chips into the fire and watched it shrivel into nothingness. "'We have a new listener with us tonight, a young lady by the name of Lisa Cairns,'" the disc jockey screeched. "'Let's give Lisa a call and see how she likes WRIP 1313, the oldest listened to radio station at night. Remember, we're the station that finds you on your radio dial. A.M. or F.M., it doesn't matter to us.' The radio went dead. A sudden chill invaded my room as I sat there on my bed, watching the phone in terror." She leaned in closer to the fire. "I don't know what I feared the most," Lisa said, "a call from a radio station that may be operated by the living dead, or the telephone waking my parents up at two in the morning. Several minutes passed and my palm started to sweat as I gripped the phone, dreading the slightest vibration. But there was no ringing, not even a little static or hum, just empty, dead air."

John looked at Rich, trying to read his reaction to Lisa's story, but he was intently staring into the climbing flames. He smiled as Lisa shifted around and stretched her legs, rubbed her temples, and arched her back. She seemed to be adjusting herself at both ends. She was drop-dead gorgeous but her normally content face now looked constricted. It stirred up memories of his summer job loading vending machines at the V.A. hospital. Everyday brought a new group of haunted soldiers who would never stop serving their country. His boss told him that most of them had finally seen more death and terror than the human mind could handle, and the only thing war had given them was a life full of dark visions. Lisa looked like she could be seeing some similar dark visions.

"I began to think that maybe it was some twisted station from New York City, because I have heard that A.M. radio signals could travel hundreds of miles if there were no other stations broadcasting at the same frequency. I figured since most A.M. stations switched off at night, that it probably was some pirate radio show, put on by a bunch of drunken college kids. I stood up and walked over to turn off my stereo. As soon as my finger touched the power switch, I heard a ringing, but it wasn't my phone. I listened closely and realized it was coming from my speakers. No other sound anywhere, only the relentless ringing of a phone. I turned off the radio, turned off my lights, and climbed into bed. Thoughts of sugarplums weren't dancing in my head, but it was late and after a few minutes, I started to doze off. When the ringing in my speakers started again, I nearly burst out of my skin.

"This is precisely why I only listen to c.d.'s," Rich said and chuckled.

"Next time you're looking for a new c.d., why don't you check the Self Help section," John said and smiled, glad to see him out of his trance. He stood up and headed toward the large woodpile; as he did, he urged her to go on.

"I sat there in the darkness of my bedroom, staring in the direction of the stereo but the radio dial wasn't glowing. The ringing went on and on. I kept listening to see if my parents were moving around but the entire world seemed to be dead. The ringing was driving me crazier than my terror, or I never would have done it," Lisa said.

"Let me guess. You turned the radio back on," Rich said.

A sudden wind sent a flurry of red leaves drifting to the ground, some of them landing in the flames and disintegrating in seconds. Crunchy leaves blew all around them, forming small piles against the circle of stones that surrounded the fire pit.

"Don't tell me you woke your mom and dad," John said and threw some chunks of rotten wood on the fire.

"I picked up my phone, but there was no dial tone. That's when I freaked."

"Tell the rest of it," John said and smiled. "We only have so much wood."

"My radio switched on by itself. I threw down the phone, and started to go wake up my parents. When I heard a voice coming from the earpiece, I immediately froze. 'Hello, is anybody out there?' it said. It repeated the same thing; only this time I heard it through the speakers. The dead air had ended.

"'We're trying to reach Lisa Cairns, is she there?' the disc jockey said. I slowly picked up my phone and listened, trying to slow my breathing and keep the mouth piece covered at the same time."

Lisa twisted her long hair and paused for a

moment as she stared into the flames.

"'She's finally answered, radio land. So tell us Lisa, how do you like our station so far?'

What kind of station is this, I asked him, more out of reaction than forethought.

'No big surprise I guess, just the same old wasted question. Hey, let's not give her flack; weren't we all like her once, unable to see past our most immediate desires and concerns.'"

"How did they know your name, and how did they get your phone number?" Rich asked.

"That's what I asked him. He said 'I've had your number for a long time, but you'll only get ours when you tell someone about us.'

What's that supposed to mean? I asked. 'Have you ever heard of being at the wrong place at the wrong time?'

Yes, I believe I've heard that concept.

'Well then, you have arrived. Now if you tell anyone else about it, you'll soon boost our ratings every night. By the way, New York City couldn't put out this kind of quality programming if the Statue Of Liberty had a brain and was president of C.B.S. Nice talking to you, Lisa. Tune in anytime. Now let's listen to the death of one of our faithful listeners as he falls off his boat while relieving himself into Lake Erie. What a ratings booster night.' It sounds crazy I know."

"Are you sure you didn't say something about them being a pirate radio show out of New York?" Rich rubbed his forehead, as if that could help clear his mind and help him figure it all out. "It is possible they could have gotten your name and number from some list."

"But how would they have known she was listening to their station?" John said. He watched Rich twist on the bench, lean forward, then back.

"Before I turned off the radio again, I heard a man drowning, and like before, I could vividly picture the scene in my mind. I could hear his fingernails scratching against the the side of the boat, desperate to reach safety. While he choked on water and gasped for air, his drunken friends yelled for help and stumbled all over the place trying to grab him. I turned off my radio, then unplugged it and my phone. I crawled into bed and tried to think about Christmas, and shopping the next day, but I kept hearing pieces of that show playing again and again, and now they knew who I was and what I was thinking. Two weeks passed before I got a good night's sleep."

"It's 11:52," Rich said. "I bet we could find this station at exactly midnight."

"I would like to find out where that station's coming from," John said. "I bet Rich is right. I bet it was midnight when you tuned in."

"So you're really going to try this?" Lisa

asked.

"Why not," Rich said.

"Because, they'll know I told you."

"My midnight theory is probably wrong anyway," Rich said. "Chances are, you'll never find that station again."

John looked at Lisa's face, and he thought he saw not only concern, but worry. "Maybe we shouldn't. She may have stumbled onto something supernatural, and if so, maybe they would know that she told us about it, and that couldn't be good.

"You can try it if you want to, but I need to head home," Lisa said and stood up.

"If it bothers you that much, we won't do it," Rich conceded

"That's alright, it's been a long night, and tomorrow will be a long day. I've got to get the place ready for all the trick or treaters." She walked around the fire pit and through the opening between the benches, and stopped at the two large fodder shocks that formed an entrance into the camp area. She turned around and said, "Thanks for putting up with me."

John stood up and set his cider down on the bench. "I'll walk you to your car."

"That's not necessary. It's only a little way, I'll be fine," Lisa said and gave John a kiss on the cheek and told Rich good-bye.

John thought of insisting, but he didn't want to seem pushy. He had figured out a couple of months ago that Lisa would probably never be more than a friend, but part of him still did not want to accept that fact. "Are you sure?"

"Really, it's o.k. Besides, Rich might get scared if you leave him here all alone."

Rich laughed. "You're pretty cool for a female," he said. "Remember, the compact disc is our friend."

"I'll never forget that," Lisa said, and then she vanished into the darkness between the campsite and the barn driveway beyond the field.

"I have to admit, that story was strange," Rich said.

"This whole area is strange," John said. "It's like everyone has at least one ghost story to tell."

"Trouble is, all stories are not true, no matter how honest the storyteller may be," Rich said. "Don't get me wrong, I don't think she lied. I think she slept through the whole thing." He stood to stretch.

"Are we still going to try to find that station?"

"I was just screwing with her. If that station existed, we would've heard about it by now. I've never heard a legend about it, not even on the Internet," Rich said.

"It's still hard to believe she dreamed the whole thing."

Rich looked at him and smiled. "Try to find it then." He sat back down and propped his brown Wolverine boots up on the warm ring of rocks. He looked at his watch. "Better hurry though, less than two minutes until midnight."

John could faintly hear Lisa start her car and drive off down Tucker Road. He wondered how the universe went about picking those that would experience life's mysteries, and the more elite crowd that would live to tell of them. Death never stops affecting the survivors, because they know it's coming for them someday, too. If we mourn the dead, we should bestow sympathy on the survivors.

"Are you ready yet?" Rich asked.

John looked down at the radio, a cloud full of mildew smelling smoke drifting over him. "You turn it on, I don't think I can."

"You'll make somebody a wonderful wife someday." Rich sprung up from the log bench and turned on the radio, to a.m. 1313. Cracks and pops shot out from the fire pit as the moist poplar surrendered to the flames. The radio was silent. "I guess that shoots down my theory or her story."

"Are you sure it's on the right station? Try tuning it in some more," John urged him.

"It should be the same position as 105, remember?"

Before Rich could turn the dial, a voice blared out from the speakers. "Good evening everybody. Our first moonlight tale is about a listener turned promoter. She first heard us a few years ago, and tonight she finally broke down and shared her secret. Right now she is on her way home, but an unexpected guest is about to give her a shock near an extremely sharp curve at the top of a very steep hill."

"Wait a minute, what is this," Rich said.

"There's the ghost now," the man on the radio said. "She sees it. She's watching it faithfully. I don't know about you folks, but surprise and terror always look so similar on a person's face, especially at night."

John leaned toward the radio, trying to hear every detail, hoping to spot a clue that may tell him this was all a sick joke, though he found it hard to imagine Lisa would play a trick like this. He heard screeching tires, a loud thump, then the crashing sounds of what sounded like a car rolling over repeatedly as it shot down a hill. She could have been to the curvy point of the road overlooking Dark Valley about now.

"Ouch, that was nasty," the voice from the radio said. "At least she is still conscious enough to enjoy the lovely fire, her second one tonight. Is it irony or is it justice? As always, you be the judge."

"This can't be real," Rich said.

"I pray you're right."

"Pray all you want to John, but your only salvation now will be your silence. Shall we introduce you to our audience?" the disc jockey said.

"This has to be Lisa's idea of a practical joke," Rich said. "Maybe she has some old Mr. Microphone or something and someone's hiding in the woods, listening to everything we say."

"Only the obituaries will truly convince these bright boys, the last living members of the Camp Fire Club. Perhaps a short introduction will hold their attention. John and Rich are familiar with haunted houses, and evil spirits. I also have a feeling they'll be listeners for a very long time. After all, we are the oldest listened to station at night. Now let's go back to the fiery scene, live, and hear Lisa's final, tormented screams as she dies for the enjoyment of the Camp Fire Club. Happy Halloween, boys."

John froze in terror, mesmerized by the flames of her burning car and her screams. She had been right, you could see the person dieing all too vividly in your mind. Rich walked over to one of the benches and sat down, burying his face in his hands. John soon followed.

"It doesn't make the images go away," Rich said.

"We can't ever tell anyone else about this," John said as he tilted back his head and stared blankly up at the moving shadows in the trees surrounding the fire pit. The radio volume increased. "Oh, god, turn it off. Take out the batteries, throw it in the fire, anything. Just make it stop."

Rich stood up and faced the radio, but paused as if afraid to get any closer. "Let's go home and just leave it here."

"Don't worry," the D.J. said, "we'll never stop waiting here for you; and we'll never stop listening for you."

John immediately stood up and started walking toward the field. As he walked between the same fodder shocks Lisa had only minutes earlier, tears burst from his eyes. He would never see her again. His last memory of Lisa would be her final screams.

Soon they would fade into dead air.

Campfire In The Dark Woods

Don't you just love October nights," Adam said as he shuffled through a pile of autumn leaves.

"Especially when you don't have to get up and go to school the next day," Scott said.

"I don't mind school," Bruce said and zipped up his L.L. Bean coat. "It gives me time to catch up on my sleep."

They all laughed as they continued walking along the edge of the forest. Light from nearby campfires cast tall shadows against the orange and red canopy of leaves.

"Why don't we get back on the road? I can hardly see where I'm walking," Adam said.

"Are you still scared of the woods?" Bruce asked.

"He's just scared of the dark now," Scott said and nudged Adam with his elbow, a wide grin on his face.

"You guys are hilarious," Adam said looking down. "Doesn't all that darkness freak you guys out at all, especially this close to Halloween?"

"Not really, since I don't believe in ghosts," Scott said. "But I admit things do feel kind of weird in late October."

"Before you guys go all Sci Fi Channel on me, look there," Bruce said and pointed into the dark forest.

Adam looked and saw what appeared to be the glow of a campfire emanating from below a small hill. "I don't remember ever seeing campsites that far down in the woods. There's no road leading there."

"Maybe it's a new primitive campsite," Scott said.

"Scioto doesn't have any primitives or my dad would've rented one of them. You guys don't know how lucky you are to have campers," Bruce said as a cool breeze lifted from within the woods. "It's not camping unless you're in a tent, says my dad Daniel Boone.

"It could be an illegal fire. We should let the rangers know," Adam said.

"Yeah, or it could be a fun party," Bruce said. "Come on, let's go find out."

Scott and Bruce headed into the thick woods, but Adam just stood there. "Let's go back guys. It's late, and I think I see fog rolling in over there."

"Come on Adam. It's not that far," Scott said.

"If anything bad happens, me and Scott will yell and you can scream for help like a girl."

"Very funny. Maybe you can replace Conan when he replaces Leno," Adam said. "I'm not afraid of the dark, I just hate darkness. I like to be able to see things."

"All kidding aside, he is right. It's only a few hundred feet. People would hear us," Scott said. "Come on, let's just see what's going on and then we'll go back to our campsites."

"I have a bad feeling about this," Adam said.

"There could be some single girls there if it is a party."

"If there's not, I'm leaving," Adam said. He stepped into the woods and close to Bruce and Scott.

They had barely started walking through the crunchy fallen leaves of the forest when the sound of girls talking filled the air.

Bruce put his arm on Adam and whispered, "I told you this was worth checking out."

Adam smiled in relief. Maybe this wouldn't be so horrible after all. The air grew colder with each step they took and fog suddenly rose up from the ground, crawling around their legs. Something told Adam none of this was normal, yet the girls at the campfire sounded fine, so how could any of them be in any real danger. Even though he had put on a brave face for the guys, the world was full of too many weirdo's. If anything out of the ordinary happened, he would scream for help just as Bruce had said. Still, it would take someone a minute or more to get to them, but the noise would probably scare off any weirdo's and save them from certain death. Of course, most murders took less than a minute to complete.

Then they were just to the edge of the light of the campfire in the woods. There around the dimly burning fire and gently rolling fog, stood three beautiful girls. Adam couldn't look away from the petite brunette who was stoking the fire. The taste of damp smoke drifted across his tongue as he whispered to Scott, "I'll take the brunette."

"Looks like we're having company again girls," the red headed one said.

"We didn't mean to scare you," Bruce said as he walked over to the blonde girl, followed by Scott. A moment later, Adam eased over next to the brunette. "We saw your fire and thought we'd drop in."

"Most Octobers, few if any come to visit, especially at night, yet you're the second group tonight," the blonde girl said.

"I'm Bruce, and this is . . ."

The blonde stopped him. "We don't care about names. Names can't keep you warm on a cold October night." She slid her arms around Bruce's neck and leaned up to kiss him.

"She's right. It takes a warm body," the red head said and began kissing Scott. The fog seemed to thicken and engulf them until they became shrouded shadows.

"This has never happened before," Adam said and stepped backward to get a little distance between him and the brunette. She was gorgeous, but girls this easy had to have something wrong with them.

The brunette moved closer, reaching out her arms. "We don't want to be left out," she said, staring deeply into his eyes.

"I'm not into easy girls like my friends," Adam said, backing away. "Getting a shot of penicillin on Monday is not my idea of fun."

"At least give me a kiss goodbye," the brunette said as the fog around them now thickened.

Adam took one more step back into the darkness and fell backwards over a stone. The brunette leaned over him. As he maneuvered away from her, he saw what had tripped him. It was a tombstone. The fog lifted up away from the ground as if a wind had blown away a cloud of smoke. He looked over at his friends, now only vaguely immersed in fog, and saw they no longer embraced beautiful girls, but hideous skeletons with rotting flesh clinging to their bones. He opened his mouth to scream but his tongue felt frozen in ice. Then the brunette, still beautiful, grabbed him with appalling strength and began kissing him. Her flesh began to wrinkle and decay as he struggled to get free. Her tongue twisted as maggots emerged from it. Bruce and Scott squirmed less and less until finally giving up their fight. The blonde pulled Bruce down into the ground. A moment later, the red head pulled Scott down into the ground, down into their graves. The fog lowered again, as quickly as it had risen before, and was sucked down into ground behind them.

Adam remembered his pledge to himself to scream for help, but he couldn't scream with a worm-infested tongue wiggling inside his mouth. The taste of rotten, damp, dirty meat filled his mouth. He was trying to scream for help, but her mouth snuffed out his pleas.

This can't be happening, he thought as terror rushed through his nerves. He felt her boney hands rip across his cheeks as they fell to the ground. His head struck a tombstone, somehow he knew it was her tombstone, and he felt her mouth pull away from his as they started sinking into her grave. It would be his grave too if he didn't scream for help. They were only a few hundred feet away from the other campers, only a minute away from help. Insane terror burned in his veins as the fog around the corpse on top of him grew as white as her bones. She rose up, her skull twisting on her boney neck, her mouth opening and shutting, clicking her teeth together. She leaned on him with her arms, pushing him down into the earth.

He opened his mouth to scream, but cold gritty rocks pressed against his teeth as his mouth filled with dirt and she forced him deep into her grave, deep into eternal darkness.

Trick Or Treat Pond

"This is a great place for a campfire," Dan said to Sean. "I didn't know there was a pond back here."

"I like it. It's quiet and secluded. There aren't any neighbors to complain if we make too much noise," Sean threw another slab of wood on the fire, then walked over to the cooler by Jim and pulled out another drink. "Heck, you can scream back here and not bother anybody."

"How come you never told us about this place sooner?" Jim asked.

Sean looked across the rising heat at them, then at the pond that stretched oblong through the forest for over 200 feet. A mist was forming over the water.

"I wanted to surprise you guys. When you make new friends, you hate to tell them everything about you all at once."

"Your idea of telling our parents we were going to the football game worked like a charm," Dan said.

"Always does," Sean said, then chuckled. He took a long drink, poked the fire with the fire stick. A flurry of leaves fluttered across their faces as a swift breeze kicked up. The sound of blowing leaves surrounded them and the flames of the fire leaned left, then right, then stood back up when the wind subsided.

"You better hope your girlfriend doesn't find out you did something without her or you're toast," Jim said.

"She won't find out," Dan said.

"I told Sandy I was going to my grandma's. It's the only place she won't call to check up on me," Jim said.

"You guys let yourselves get pushed around too much. If you let people boss you around, especially girls, there's no telling how you'll end up someday," Sean said, glancing at the pond.

"I'm not scared of her, I just don't want to argue about it," Dan said.

"I just want things to go nice and easy if you know what I mean," Jim said.

"My grandpa was a lot like you guys, that's why he put up with my grandma's crap his entire life. Anything he loved, she hated. When he started bringing me here to fish, she couldn't stand to see him happy, so one day she started dumping expired farm chemicals in the pond. You name the herbicide, pesticide, or fertilizer, and my grandma dumped it in the water. Pretty soon we were catching two headed fish. When grandpa found out what she had done, they had a huge fight, but she always managed to justify her actions.

"Sounds like fishing in there's out of the question," Jim said

"Fish can't survive in that water anymore. My grandpa had had enough and wanted to teach grandma a lesson. He was going to take whatever he caught and feed it to her, so one night, he went out in the rowboat to do some fishing, but he fell overboard and they never found his body."

"You telling me your grandpa's still in that pond somewhere?" Dan asked.

"He sure is. I know it to be a fact. Just like I know you two are too scared to go out on the pond in his old boat," Sean said.

"I came for an October campfire. It's too late in the year to go boating," Jim said, looking up from the glowing embers.

"I figured you two would be afraid to go out on the water since you're both scared of your girlfriends. But hey, if you're not ashamed to admit your fear to everyone back at school, more power to you."

"He might be a whipped prep, but I'm not afraid to go across that pond," Dan said. "In fact, I'm pretty sure you're making this whole story up just to freak us out since tomorrow's Trick or Treat."

Jim laughed. "You had me going there for a minute. Why would you have campfires right next to the place where your grandpa died?" Jim stood up and zipped his leather coat. "You're not telling everyone at school that you scared me. Where's the boat?"

Sean smiled, then walked away from the warmth of the fire and over to the edge of the pond. "Here's a row boat, but nobody ever makes it across alive. This is one time that being a chicken is O.K." Sean said.

Dan looked at him with a cocky grin and sat down in the rowboat, followed by Jim. The smell of muddy water and earthworms mixed with the bitter smoke of the nearby campfire. "Shove us off."

Sean pushed the rowboat away from the banks into the mist crawling across the water. "Trick or Treat boys."

"Hey, aren't you coming?" Jim asked.

"Grandpa doesn't like me to go in the pond. He says it's too dangerous."

"I thought you said your grandpa was dead," Jim said looking over the side of the boat with concern at the bubbling water.

"I think you're story is all bull," Dan said. "If you thought you were going to scare me, you're going to be disappointed."

"Dan, there's something moving in -"
The boat flipped up in the air and turned over, dumping Jim and Dan into the dark

waters of the pond. Dan screamed for help in a high-pitched voice and Jim swore as fast as he could. A moment later, sharp teeth ripped pieces of flesh from their bodies until their minds surrendered to death. Pools of blood floated in the center of the lake.

From somewhere within the mist over the water came the voice of Sean's grandpa.

"Very tasty. Not quite the meal your grandma was, but that should do me for a few weeks." The water stirred and sloshed. "That's why I left my fortune to you; I knew you'd never forget your old grandpa."

"I play a trick and you get a treat, grandpa."

The mutated creature Sean's grandpa had become, sank down into the murky water and burrowed its slimy body several feet below the bottom of the pond.

Sean headed back to the football game as cold October fog rolled past him. He zipped up his Italian leather jacket. Grandpa leaving him all that money made everything in life easier, especially finding new friends.

Cabin Above The Dead

A dark cloud devoured the late after-noon sun on Labor Day weekend, sending shadows running for shelter at Gullette Grove campground. The sweating sunbathers seemed to welcome the sudden shade, unaware of the terror about to be unleashed upon them.

Rick Evans moved his binoculars left, then right. "Man, I don't know which one should be the future Mrs. Evans. The blonde's built, but the girl in the red bikini is tough."

Tony Hines adjusted his set of binocu-lars away from the beach and over to the diving board in the middle of the lake. "You obviously have not seen the cute red head

I'm gonna be meeting in about 10 minutes."

"You guys are like two old perverts watching girls in the park," Aaron said as he threw a towel around his neck.

"Except these girls are barely dressed and we're not old," Tony said.

"That cemetery above the beach is weird. Why would they bury people so close to a campground?" Rick remarked.

"If you look close by that pine forest, you'll see a mausoleum. What a view for the dead," Tony said.

"From the look of the sky, none of us are going to get to swim today," Jerry said as he flicked his orange yo-yo again. "Just as well, those girls won't be interested in any of us. If I had known there was a grave-yard this close, I never would've come to this campground."

"You're so lame man. Those girls have to hook up with someone this weekend. It might as well be us," Rick said.

"Jerry won't kiss a girl until one holds him down and forces herself on him," Aaron said as he leaned over Rick's shoulder to look out the cabin window at the clouds. "He is right. I think it's going to-"

A huge blast of lightning burst from the sky and struck the mausoleum roof, send-ing chunks of concrete flying. The people on the beach scrambled to gather their things, while swimmers hurried ashore.

Three more bolts hit the cemetery over-looking the lake. Thunder rattled the glass windows in their cabin and heavy rain-drops pounded the tin roof.

Rick moved his gaze away from the babe in the red bikini to the burning tree in front of the mausoleum. "I hope the rain puts that out."

"What the ---," Tony's mouth fell open and his hands grew too weak to hold up his binoculars. He stared across the beach, up to the hillside cemetery directly across from their hill, his hands shaking.

"What's wrong?" Jerry said, still playing with his yo-yo. "I knew something was going to go wrong this weekend."

"What?" Rick said and turned his binoculars in the direction Tony had been looking. He saw the unspeakable. A wave of terror swept over his chest.

"Let me see," Aaron said as he took Tony's binoculars and looked in the direction of the cemetery.

Rick dropped his binoculars and walked away from the window. "There's no way what I just saw could happen. No way. He sat down on the couch, feeling dazed.

Aaron's own jaw dropped when he saw with horrible clarity the nightmare visions that had shaken his friends. "That's impossible," he whispered.

Jerry tossed his yo-yo on the cooler and walked over to look out the window. Aaron handed him the binoculars. A moment later, the front of Jerry's shorts had a dark, wet stain. "They're climbing out of their graves. Those things are walking toward the beach. Is this some prank you guys arranged?"

No one answered him.

"Zombies aren't real, at least that's what we've been told by our parents and teachers our whole lives," Rick said.

"I guess they were wrong," Aaron replied.

"We've got to get out of here!" Jerry yelled.

"He's right. If they eat people like in the movies, this ain't the place to spend our last wild weekend before college starts," Tony said.

"They eat people?" Jerry whined. "Mom warned me not to come up here with you guys." He ran over and locked the door.

"And my Mom made me ask you to come because we're second cousins and she feels sorry for you," Aaron said.

"Let's not lose it guys," Tony said.

"But the only road out of here goes right past the beach," Rick replied.

"I'm not going anywhere near those things," Jerry said. "Maybe if we just hide, they'll fill up on other people and leave."

A final hush fell over the room, as they each seemed to be working out solutions and rational explanations at the same time. A blast of thunder destroyed the silence, only the pounding did not end when it should have. Someone, or something, was pounding on their cabin door. When the thumping stopped, then started again, everyone jumped. A piercing scream of a woman sliced through the air.

"Let us in please! I have a child! They're coming to get us!" She pounded frantically again. "They're almost here. They're faster than in the movies." Her pounds and pleas subsided into sobs and whimpering. "Don't let us die like that."

By the time Tony reached the door to open it, she ran off the porch to the cabin next door, shouting hysterical pleas.

"We can't let her in anyway. She may be one of them," Jerry said.

Rick picked up the binoculars and looked down at the beach. What he saw made him vomit against the glass.

Aaron went to him and looked himself. He understood Rick's reaction. Only half-eaten pieces of the swimmers remained. He saw a torso with a red bikini top and nothing more. It was Thanksgiving Day for zombies. Then a faint smell of death and decayed, rotten flesh crawled into his nose and wouldn't leave. He felt his own stomach turn. When he lowered his binoculars, he saw at least twenty zombies, each in a feeding frenzy rage, climbing the hill to the cabins. "We have less than a minute, they're coming for us." They heard the woman next door, banging on that cabin door, pleading to let her inside. "They'll be here before she realizes it," Aaron said. "Those people aren't going to answer, they were on the beach."

Jerry pulled his shirt up over his face. "What's that smell, it's making me sick."

Tony looked out the kitchen window at her. "She's not a zombie. We better let her in. She's got a little girl with her."

Jerry blocked the door with his body. "You're not opening this door for anyone. Aaron said they're coming. She'll be fine in that cabin."

The guys surrounded Jerry and threw him onto the couch. Aaron walked over to the door, opened it and shouted to her. "Hurry, in here."

She ran, dragging the little girl part of the way. When she was half way to their cabin, Aaron looked to his left and saw three zombies fast approaching the wooden porch of their cabin. He looked right at the woman pulling on the child's hand. She was farther away from the porch than the zombies, and running half as fast. The little girl was weeping. Aaron looked back over his left shoulder again at the decayed, ravenous zombies. They locked eyes and the biggest zombie opened his mouth, out fell the rest of the little red bikini. Without thinking, he ran off the porch toward the woman and picked up her little girl. He ran as fast as he could. "Run, Run!"

"Oh God, we're not going to make it!" she screamed.

"Hurry," Tony yelled as he held the door.

The first zombie started to climb onto the porch. Aaron ran inside with the girl

70

and set her down as the big zombie stood and started walking toward them. He only needed four more steps to reach the door.

"Shut the door," Jerry screamed from inside. "Shut the door, they'll eat us alive!"

The woman climbed onto the porch and stood face to face with the big zombie when she reached the doorway. Two more zombies moaned while ascending the two steps onto the porch, reaching out their bloody hands for her.

The big zombie grabbed for the woman but she ducked, fell to the floor and rolled inside the doorway. Tony slammed the door and reached for the lock, but all three zombies were now at the door twisting the handle. "Help me!" Tony moaned. Aaron reached up and together they twisted the doorknob slowly until Tony turned the lock. Aaron then reached up and slid the chain lock on the door.

The woman held her child and they both rocked in each other's arms. The woman kept repeating, "Thank you, thank you," in a low, whimpering voice.

"You guys are idiots!" Jerry yelled as Rick let him loose from the headlock.

"Sorry, but I couldn't let you slam the door on our friends," Rick said to Jerry in disgust.

"You should've run track," Tony said.

"I wasn't fast enough," Aaron said and they laughed.

A jolting pounding on the door broke

71

the momentary terror reprieve. The woman and little girl jumped in unison.

"Don't make us force our way in. You can't block all the windows you know," a zombie said from outside.

"They talk too? They never talk in the movies," Rick said.

"Start pulling anything you can in front of the windows," Tony said to the guys.

"Listen, we've nearly had our fill. We just want one more snack before we move on," the zombie said.

Jerry and Rick pulled couches, chairs and mattresses against the windows while Aaron tried to comfort the woman and her child.

The zombies all laughed. "A couch isn't going to keep us out, but we're in no mood for a fight. Death can be quite tiring. Throw out one person and we'll be on to easier prey."

Another zombie spoke, "Come on mister, save us all a bunch of trouble. We need more food to stay alive long enough to get to our next buffet. We aren't stopping here. What's it going to be, one of you, or all of you?

"They're going to get us after all," the little girl cried.

"Throw one of them out," Jerry said. "They'd both be dead now anyway if it wasn't for you idiots."

"If anyone's going out, it should be me, not my little girl! Please don't give her to those monsters."

"I can't believe no one's cell phone works here. Maybe you should try them again," Jerry urged.

"This is a dead zone. You can't even get one bar out here," the woman said.

"We're stepping away to show you there's no tricks. Just give us something to eat and we'll leave," a voice from outside spoke.

"All the other zombies are leaving out the exit road toward town it looks like," Rick said. "Maybe they would leave."

"We can't just throw someone to their death, especially that kind of death," Aaron said.

"He's right. How would we pick? Besides, they could be bluffing," Tony said. "Why would they settle for just one when they could easily bust in here and have all six of us?"

"I'd pick the woman. We don't know her. It's not our job to save her," Jerry said.

"Why don't you just shut up," Aaron said.

"Look, maybe they're not that strong. They are animated corpses and from the looks of them, they've been dead a while. But even that little girl could break in here if she was willing to go to all the effort," Rick said.

Just then, the glass of the two front windows exploded.

"My friend's a little impatient when he's

hungry," the zombies shouted.

"Your right," the woman said. "They're going to kill us all unless one of us goes out. I don't want my daughter to die that way and she's so young." She looked at the door with terror in her eyes. "I'll go."

"No, mom!" the little girl said as she clutched her mom tight around the neck.

"It's O.K. honey. It's the only way. You go home to Grandma's and be a good girl." She stood up to meet her destiny. The little girl grabbed her legs. Tony pulled the little girl free and held her as she kicked and twisted.

"It's alright Megan, mommy loves you, always remember that."

"What's your name?" Aaron asked. "I never knew your name."

She smiled at him, "Charity. My name is Charity McQuay."

"Hurry up Charity, before those things bust in here and make hamburger out of your little girl," Jerry said.

The little girl went limp and sobbed. Charity cried and slid off the chain lock, then reached for the knob. "I love you Megan."

"Wait," Aaron said. "If we're going to do this, if we're going to have this on our shoulders the rest of our lives that we sacrificed someone to save ourselves, it can't be you, Charity. You're a mom."

"He's right," Rick said. "I'll go in your place."

"Your parents would be torn up man," Tony said. "My dad hasn't even seen me in five years and mom never even notices me. I should go."

"Guys, I brought her here, it really should be me," Aaron said somberly.

"I don't care who it is, just as long you hurry. They look angry," Jerry said. "If it was me, I'd send the kid. She could always have another one."

A sudden, knowing glance passed in that instance between Rick, Aaron and Tony.

"You know Jerry, if we're going to feed those creatures, why give them sweet meat when we could give them something spoiled?" Aaron said.

"You're wasting time," Jerry snapped. "We don't have any meat here except hot dogs."

Tony and Rick moved toward Jerry's legs as Aaron grabbed his arms. They carried Jerry toward the door, twisting and jerking.

"Even though you're heartless, this isn't easy," Aaron said. "My mom will be really mad if she ever finds out, but it's the only way."

"If it was just us guys, we'd all go down together," Rick said.

"But we can't let them die," Tony said, motioning to Charity and Megan.

"Put me down you jerks! You can't do this to me."

"Could you open the door Charity?"
Aaron asked.

"There's got to be another way," she
pleaded.

"No!" Jerry screamed. "Send the kid,
not me."

Meagan stepped in front of her mom
and opened the door as she watched Jerry
with fear in her eyes. The zombies rushed
toward the cabin.

"Make it quick," Aaron pleaded.

They tossed Jerry onto the front porch,
then slammed the door. A second later,
Jerry scratched and clawed at the door.

"I'm sorry guys. Please let me in.
Please- "

Then the sound of steps on the front
porch, followed by what seemed like an
eternity of screams. They heard several
loud snapping sounds and finally the
screams ended. Then the chewing sounds
began. Everyone covered their ears to block
out the chomping and slurping. "God forgive us," Aaron said with tears in his eyes.

Twenty minutes later, after the zombies had left, they all and climbed out the
back window to avoid seeing what was left
of Jerry; though in time, they would each
create their own dark vision in the realm of
their nightmares.

Monster Lake

Alarge shadow swept over rangers John and Mark as a large storm cloud swallowed up the bulk of the early evening light. They drove by the campsites along the lake's edge as campers tended fires and cooked dinner before the storm hit. Tarps and screen houses shading picnic tables breathed in and out like a dieing animal struggling to breathe. A STOP THE D.O.E. NUCLEAR WASTE KILLS sign flapped back and forth in front of an RV campsite.

"Nuclear waste has brought back 1,200 good paying jobs for people from Greenfield to Portsmouth," Mark said.

"What good are jobs if everyone ends

up with cancer," John said. "The plant sits right over a branch of the largest aquifer in the country. Seems foolish to risk poisoning our country's water supply."

"We'll all be better off financially as time goes by. Besides, Washington has guaranteed it will be easy to contain it."

John heard a distant rumble nearby. "I'm still shocked a forest ranger working on a lake down stream from the nuclear plant could be so supportive of such an unsustainable and unsafe energy product."

"Hey, it's cleaner than coal Mr. Green Peace."

"Until you have all the radioactive waste to deal with for the next million years," John said and rolled his window down for some air. "Face it, the nuclear lobbyists have more money and friends in politics than the wind and solar industry."

"Let the next generation deal with the side effects. An asteroid could hit the Earth in the next thirty years and what would it matter then?"

John shook his head and looked away from Mark. He had no right being in forestry. "You're a real-"

Several rapid gunshots shattered the relative silence of the campground. John pushed down on the peddle of the Bronco and headed toward the sound.

"I think it came from down at the west docks," Mark said, now leaning forward in his seat.

A moment later, they pulled up to the docks where ranger Fred Stevens stood staring down at the end of the dock into the water. John and Mark jumped out and ran over to him, rocking the floating dock and making splashing sounds in the water as they did.

"What the -"

"Do you still believe Washington can easily contain the waste?" John asked as he stared at Mark's terrified and confused face, then back at the lake's unusually green water, then back at the new species.

Even though the water was about fifteen feet deep at the end of the dock, at least two feet of the dead creature's body stuck up out of the lake. Streaks of dim, glowing green liquid mixed with the blood that still oozed from the gun shot wounds.

"I came down here because I heard two boys screaming bloody murder. I got here just as it rose up out of the lake and swallowed most of their kayak, with them in it." Fred swallowed hard and looked at John with wide-eyed horror. "Then it headed for me, so I unloaded on it."

His eyes still wide with disbelief, Mark said, "It's huge. It's bigger than the Bronco."

"You're just seeing the front half of it too. The rest of it is under the deeper water out there," Fred said.

John felt a mix of anger and horror swell up inside him as he stared at what could only be a result of some type of massive radioactive genetic mutation. For such mutations to occur at all, the potency of the uranium spilled had to be a hundred times worse than the Department of Energy had described.

"We trusted them," Mark said and looked at John and Fred. "I trusted them. Global warming wasn't a problem, and nuclear waste could be stored safely. I've defended it all, now look." Mark covered his face with his hands.

"Hitler got all of Germany to follow him into starting World War II. He did it by controlling and manipulating information," Fred said and placed his hand on Mark's right shoulder. "In today's world, it's even more difficult to know who's telling you the truth."

"The mouth on that thing's big enough to swallow a car, and the teeth look sharp enough to chew through it," John said.

"Judging by the fur and the short arms, I'm assuming it mixed with a bear or maybe a raccoon that came down for a drink," Fred said as he reloaded his pistol.

John felt a sudden jolt of awareness. "Every fish in the lake has probably mutated, and every animal in the woods that has drunk the water." He stroked his closed eyelids, attempting to grasp the situation. "I agree with you. That thing either started out on land and moved to the lake or somehow a fish grabbed a drinking animal and they merged. If the lake's contaminated, this whole campground is radioactive."

"Then why haven't we seen any of these animals yet, or heard any fisherman asking about the strange new fish?" Mark asked. "How come none of us are sick?"

Fred looked down at the circular waves caused by the first droplets of rain hitting the lake. He appeared unable to look at either of them. "The answer to that is as unbelievable as it is terrifying." He rubbed his temple methodically. "I checked the water for pollutants and bacteria four days ago, and everything was fine."

"That means this has all happened in a matter of days, maybe even hours?" Mark asked.

"I'm afraid so," Fred said.

"That means this nightmare has just begun and we need to evacuate this campground immediately and make sure no water escapes from the dam," John said. "Come on, let's hurry."

Fred and Mark followed him to the Bronco.

"If that's what a fish looks like, what's going to happen to raccoons, snakes, oh God, what about the bears?" Fred asked.

"We'll never be able to come back here again. This campground is now officially closed forever," John said.

"We're not the only lake being fed from the plant site neither," Fred said.

"We have to notify the Governor first

thing," John said as he exceeded the usual speed limit, honking his horn to warn any roaming campers.

"What about the campers? The Governor can wait," Fred said.

"If the waste has leaked into the creeks, then it's in the aquifer by now." John turned on the wipers.

"That means half the people in this country could be exposed to this soon, if they're not already," Fred said.

"Judging from the looks of that thing back there, people dieing would not be the worst of it," John said. He rounded the corner and turned into the campground area.

"Just slow her down," Mark said from the back seat as he pushed the barrel of his pistol against John's head. "Go on, slow her down."

"What are you doing?" Fred asked.

"Just get on the p.a. and tell everyone a tornado has been spotted forty miles away and the campground is being evacuated. Tell them to drive north and they'll be fine."

John slowed down the Bronco and Fred grabbed the p.a. and began announcing the tornado warning.

"Mark, you are way out of line."

"The name's actually Seth and I'm just doing my job. The Department Of Energy will contain this and all will be well again. The Governor doesn't need to be bothered with this."

"Mark, or Seth, whoever you may be.

That aquifer will poison half this country."

"It will be much more diluted than this lake. Probably just a few extra birth defects and an elevated cancer death rate for a few decades, then it will be like none of this ever happened."

"So what, the D.O.E. sent you to spy on us since we were speaking out against their plan to bring the waste here in the first place?" John asked as he turned up the speed of the windshield wipers.

"Not because you spoke out, because people were actually listening and organizing behind you and the other rangers. Dissent is good for democracy as long as it's ineffectual. They knew your little group would never give up so I was sent to monitor the situation."

Fred's voice mixed with the sound of his words amplified over the loud speaker and the swishing of the windshield wipers as Mark reached up and took John's pistol from his holster. Lightning flashed and the smell of earthworms and cedar filled the air as a swift wind blew up from the lake rocking the Bronco.

"Hand over your gun," Mark said to Fred.

"I dropped it back at the dock. I guess from shock. You're welcome to check if you don't believe me."

Mark took his gun in his left hand, slid to the right, and leaned up to slide his hand between Fred's seat and the door to check his holster while doing his best to keep his gun pointed at John. "Just keep driving Johnny boy."

As Mark's slid his hand between Fred's seat & the door, John looked down at something pressing against his leg. It was Fred's gun.

"The tornado is still forty miles away, but you must evacuate now," Fred continued over the speaker.

Mark felt Fred's empty holster and smiled confidently then spoke in a mocking accent, "Folks in these parts sure are honest."

"Not always," John said as he swung himself around in his seat and met Mark with Fred's gun pointed slightly upwards so the bullet wouldn't go in the direction of any campers. He squeezed the trigger, then looked away. A deafening shot rattled the vehicle, and he saw Fred plugging his ears. A loud piercing ring coursed through his skull. He jerked the Bronco to a stop. Pain rushed through his head from the sound of the blast and everything sounded muffled. He glanced over his shoulder as fast as possible to make sure Mark was no longer a threat. He struggled to push the image of what he saw in his backseat out of his mind but he couldn't. He had killed men before in Iraq, but seldom at such close range. He hated doing it then, and he hated doing it now. He knew in his gut it was wrong, but then, as now, he did it with the consolation of ultimately saving more lives than he took.

"It had to be done. He would've killed us both and millions more, much more slowly," Fred said.

John couldn't really hear the words, but he nodded in understanding from the look of concern on Fred's face. Then something jerked Fred out of the Bronco and into the storm. When John looked down, he saw part of Fred was still inside the Bronco. He screamed, but he couldn't even hear his own screams. He grabbed the p.a. microphone and started yelling, "Get out! Get out! There's been a radioactive spill!"

When he neared the ranger station, he knew it was too late. Huge bears ripped apart motor homes and devoured screaming campers in an instant. He drove even faster, weaving around bodies and torn camper parts. Everyone in the campground was heading this way. He had to warn them. How had all this happened so quickly. It almost seemed like a coordinated attack, planned by all the creatures ruined by man's greed. But animals couldn't communicate and plan like that, at least the animals they once had been couldn't. Perhaps these new animals created by the government's infinite wisdom could do such things.

He ran over a snake like creature with the head of a catfish and it screamed like a woman as he spun the vehicle around in

the station parking lot. As soon a he was
facing the direction he had just come from,
his heart sank. Campers and trees now
blocked the road, and several three-headed
creatures with red eyes were dragging
lifeless bodies behind them and staring
straight at him. His passenger window now
broken, it wouldn't be hard for them to grab
him. He heard rattling sounds under the
Bronco and saw dozens of raccoons with
huge front teeth, glowing green eyes, and
snakes for tails rushing toward him. The
screams of people mixed with never heard
before growls, roars, and hissing sounds.
Cold rain blew in on him from the passenger side. Then out of the corner of his eye,
he saw a fast approaching thing that looked
like part deer, part rat, only it was ten feet
tall. It smashed and chomped its teeth as
it moved thirty, twenty, then ten feet from
his passenger door. He jammed his foot on
the peddle and turned the wheel as far as
it would go. The creature slammed into the
back half of the Bronco as he was taking
off. The backside glass shattered. Clangs
and clunks from underneath the Bronco
rang out as thumps and thuds showered
down on top of the roof. Every animal from
the forest seemed to be attacking him,
though he could no longer discern what
some of the animals had once been. The
Bronco fishtailed and slowed, but he never
let off the gas. He twisted the wheel in the
opposite direction, then saw the deer rat

creature in the glow of the remaining twilight about to slam through the tailgate glass. The Bronco's wheels spun faster and faster and the deer rat thing kept pace for what seemed an eternity, snorting and bellowing as if in great pain, then it faded from his rearview mirror as he sped away from the campground, dragging his rear bumper, leaving behind a trail of sparks.

John drove feverishly through the storm, slowly regaining his hearing, though the ringing persisted. He had to warn the Governor. If any of those creatures reached the dam, that water would eventually make its way to the ocean. What would that create, one hundred foot sharks mixed with squid? The water aquifer now most likely contaminated, he hoped the human population would not experience such mutations. The National Guard would have to be called up to destroy all the wildlife within at least twenty miles of the lake, or else the slaughter at the campground would continue in an ever-widening circle.

He would insist on speaking with the Governor personally. He could take no more chances on moles like Mark, or Seth, whoever the guy had really been. The Governor was the country's only hope for stopping this disaster and telling the people the truth. Yet, he had his doubts. The governor had bragged about all the jobs he created in such an impoverished area and Seth had been a state employee. Was it with the

Governor's knowledge, or had the Department of Energy merely used some smoke and mirrors or political muscle to get Seth hired?

The images of the mutated beasts and the butchered campers haunted his mind. The thought of such mutations crossing over into the human population turned his body cold. But it would happen, and more scenes like tonight would play out again if they had the Governor in their pocket too. He forced his eyes not to glance down at the remains of Fred or back at Seth's body. If anyone thought him insane, he would show them their bodies and then they would know he wasn't fooling.

He entered the capital city to search for the man who would either put an end to this nightmare, or put an end to him.

There was not much time. Those creatures still roamed the night and soon they would need to find more prey.

What if some of the smaller creatures had attached themselves to his vehicle, and were now randomly dropping off throughout the streets of the city, contaminating everything they touched, killing everyone they found? He wondered why that had not occurred to him sooner, before it was too late.

Dead Wood Cabins

We haven't seen a house or another car for ten minutes. Being in the middle of nowhere like this freaks me out," Janie Gobles said from the back seat of the Toyota minivan. She watched her father's eyes glance up at the rearview mirror to look at her momentarily.

"It's only one weekend. It will do us all good to get out of Boston and get back to nature," her dad said.

"It looks like we're going all the way back to where nature began," Bob said, then chuckled.

"You won't be laughing when some inbred cannibals murder us all," Janie said then pressed her face against her window.

Endless forests engulfed them as the canopy of branches that met over top of the road hid the sun from view.

Her mother twisted around in her seat. "That is the last I want to hear of this. Your father needs some peace and quiet and it won't kill you to spend a few days in a cabin."

"It sounds cool to me. Nine hundred acres and only eight cabins. We won't see another person at all. I plan on whizzing off the front porch every morning," Bob said.

"Eew, gross!" Janie said.

"Make sure no one else is around when you do that," her dad said.

They rounded a corner and the road narrowed from two lanes to one. They climbed a small hill then saw the tall log gates of the campground. A large, wooden sign hung over the entrance:
DEAD WOOD CABINS
"Where families can
REST IN PEACE."

As they passed under the gate and into the camp, Janie spoke up. "You've got to be kidding. Did you see that sign? Rest in peace."

"Hopefully that's what we'll do if you'll ever relax," her mom said.

"Rest in peace, R.I.P. That's what they put on tombstones."

"Settle down now. We're at the check in point," her dad said as they pulled up to a small cabin with an Office sign hanging from the front porch. He parked the Sienna in front of a small hitching post. "Janie, I want you to come with me to check in so you can see the place isn't run by inbred cannibals."

Janie slid open her door and followed him in. She nearly knocked her dad over when the screen door made a loud whack as it slammed shut. "Believe it or not, a lot of people that come here would be disappointed if the screen doors didn't do that," a short, stocky man said from behind a small wooden counter.

"My daughter's a little on edge about being so deep in the wilderness."

"Don't let all the trees fool you. You're barely an hour's drive from Bangor," the man said as he looked at her, then her dad. "That's just a guess of course, but I'm sure it's factual to say it's definitely less than three. My name's Tucker. I own this slice of heaven."

"We're the Gobles from Boston."

"You're in luck. I got you all set up in the best cabin on the grounds. It's about a half mile straight behind the office."

Janie gasped. "A half mile. Not only can't we get cell phone service, but we're half a mile away from the office."

"Relax young lady. We close the office before dark anyway. So it wouldn't make much difference if you were next door." Tucker walked over to the sidewall and grabbed the #1 cabin key. "These woods are

91

thick and get very dark at night. I make sure I'm home before then. Too many critters crawl around these parts at night."

Janie tugged her dad's LL Bean field coat. "I don't like the sound of this."

Tucker handed the key to her dad. "It's too late to worry about all that now. Just keep a good fire going at night and stay close to your cabin and you'll be gone by Saturday."

"Actually, I had booked us to stay through Sunday morning," her dad said.

Tucker stared at her dad for a moment, then smiled, though it seemed forced to her. "Yes you did."

"Well, thank you. Should we drop the key off here on Sunday or leave it in the cabin?"

"I'm usually busy on Sundays. You see, I also run a used car lot and usually dedicate Sundays to that business, so the office will be locked. But leave the key at your cabin, I'll find it once you're gone."

"Good enough," her dad said and turned to go back to the car.

Even though she was sixteen years old, she didn't care that she was clutching her dad's arm. She also wasn't ashamed when she jumped again when the screen door slammed. She looked back at Tucker, his face now shaded and muffled by the screen. He was intently staring at them. Although her glance had been too quick to be sure, she thought she also saw him smiling.

She sat quietly as they drove deeper into the woods. Halfway there, tree branches started brushing against her window as the road narrowed. Then a small clearing came into view where the cabin set, lurching like a vulture on a small rise. Nearby, a stone-encircled fire pit looked ready to burn. Several wooden benches made from logs and slabs of trees sat around the pit, along with a large cedar picnic table.

"The cabin's beautiful," her mom said.

"Why don't we send Janie in first in case there are inbred cannibals up here in this part of Maine."

Janie made a fist and punched his shoulder. "Shut up."

"You'd better settle down young lady," her mom said.

"You too Bob. Don't be trying to scare your sister. She's already on edge. Now let's have a good time. Before you know it Janie, it will all be over."

"You sound like that guy back there, only he said before you know it you'll be gone. As in dead. Resting in peace, just like the sign said," Janie said.

"What's she talking about?" her mom asked.

"Nothing. The guy was a little odd, I'll admit that, but he lives up here on a logging road, what do you expect. She's reading way too much into everything. I'm sure the sign is just good ole dry New England humor."

Bob jumped out of the van and ran up to the fire pit. "Let's get a fire going!"

"Now that's the spirit. Everybody grab something and let's get unloaded," her dad said.

Three hours later, with the dinner dishes cleaned up, the tranquility of such absolute seclusion began to work its magic even on Janie. They sat close to the fire and talked as Bob and Janie roasted marshmallows. Everyone finally seemed to be enjoying themselves when the noises began.

"What was that?" Janie asked and scooted up against her dad.

"Now don't lose your happy thought. We're in the middle of Maine, it could be anything," her dad answered.

"It's probably a moose or a bear," Bob said.

"You don't think it's a bear do you?" Janie's mom said as she got up and sat down on the other side of her husband.

"Whatever it is will be scared away by our fire," her dad said. "Why don't you throw a few more logs on there Bob. It's getting kind of cold anyway."

Bob loaded his arms up with logs from the woodpile, walked over to the fire pit and dropped them all in. A flurry of sparks shot up into the black sky and the fire temporarily dimmed before the new logs started to catch fire.

Then another loud snap from the woods

followed two muffled leaf crunches. Now Bob moved over by his dad.

"It's getting closer," Janie said as she stared into the cold blackness of the forest. The harsh smell of wood smoke mixed with the scent of pinesap and dried autumn leaves. She smelled something else, something her nose could not identify. Though it was a faint smell, its strangeness disturbed her. It reminded her of the zoo. A shiver inched up her spine as the chilly air pushed away the heat from the flames.

"What's that smell?" her mom asked.

"What if it's a Jersey Devil? They say they can kill cows," Bob said.

"There's no such thing," her dad said.

Her mom turned to her dad, "Ron, tell me this isn't the stretch of woods in Maine where all those people have vanished. Tell me you didn't take us there."

Her dad sat there in silence for a moment. "I'm not really sure. I never really checked into that."

"You've got to be kidding," Janie said.

"Most of the time lost people turn up somewhere. However, many people wander off and get lost, then die from the elements. We're not going to wander off. According to the papers, no one has ever found any dead bodies. If it was an animal killing people, surely a half eaten body would turn up somewhere."

"I thought you hadn't looked into it?" her mom said.

Another snap in the trees, this one at the edge of the fire light. "Like I said, if you don't wander off, you're in no real danger."

Her mom shook her head, "Tell me you at least brought your pistol?"

"Relax. It's up in the cabin."

Then Janie's brother shot straight up into the air like one of the sparks from the fire. He vanished just as quick. Her mother fainted and fell backward off the bench. Her dad stood up, pulling her with him.

"Dad, it got Bob!"

Her dad walked around the bench to her mom, Janie clutching his arm. "Let go Janie, I have to get your mom." He bent down and picked her up.

"Dad, what is it?"

He started walking as fast as he could, Janie holding onto the cuff of his coat.

"We have to get in the cabin. We have to get the gun. I'm going to get your brother back."

The cabin was still at least sixty feet away. She looked above their heads, but she only saw dim shadows of tree branches as they moved away from the campfire's glow. That zoo like smell pricked her nose and made her want to sneeze. How could this be happening? Her dizzy stomach boiled and gnawed at the hot dogs there and she started to feel dizzy.

The cabin looked about forty feet away. She heard the tree branches above them rustling. Twenty-five more feet and they

would be in the safety of the cabin. A hor-
rid screech, high pitched and evil tore open
their eardrums. It stopped her dad in his
tracks and he dropped her mom to cover
his ears. She slammed her hands over her
ears too and shouted. "Come on dad!" she
screamed. "Just twenty more feet."

A chewed chunk of meat and bones fell
from the sky and squished as it landed. She
screamed when she saw one of Bob's sneak-
ers attached to the gnawed up flesh. Then
in a flash, her dad flew out of her sight and
into the woods.

"No!" Janie screamed, tears pouring
down her cold cheeks. She sat in shock for
a moment, then a snapping branch jerked
her back. She hooked her arms under
her mom's and starting pulling her backward toward the cabin. She grunted as she
struggled to move her mom.

"Mom, wake up," she panted. Then
another screech and she heard a loud thud
on the roof of the cabin. She knew it was
the remains of her dad. She looked over her
shoulder for the cabin. The porch was only
ten feet away. She pulled and strained her
back, her mom's feet dragging the ground,
rustling leaves. Then her feet ran into the
front step and she fell backward. Her head
slammed into the ridge of a wooden step.
She felt consciousness slipping away. No,
not now. I'm so close. She tried to hold on,
to work through the pain. She slipped away,
then seconds (or was it minutes?) later

came to. Her mom was gone. She slipped away, then again her eyes opened. Her head pounded and throbbed. She didn't see her mom anywhere. Loneliness like she had never known settled on her heart.

I have to get inside she thought. I have to warn other people. She sat up slowly on her elbows, and her eyes gradually focused in on the blazing campfire below. The flames twisted, rose, and fell in random flashes of orange and white. Then the flashes vanished and it took her a moment to realize through her grogginess that actually something had blocked them from her view. Something from the cold blackness of the forest.

The smell overwhelmed her and she felt a single long strand of cold saliva drip onto her forehead, and run down between her nose and her eyes across her lips. It was her first taste of death.

Before she could fully focus in on what was about to devour her, the teeth were coming down to clamp around her face. She screamed. What good is a scream if no one is around to hear it she thought. Muffled screams turned to silent gasps as the creature's mouth enveloped the front of her skull.

The next morning, Tucker cleaned up the campsite and burned the remainder of the Goble's belongings. Cleaning up the blood stains and remains took the longest. He made quick work of it because seven more campsites needed cleaned up before darkness fell. Being in the woods after dark was risky, and campfires really drew those things in too, especially in October, just before hibernation, but he would be home long before dark. He drove the Toyota Sienna into a trailer and drove it twenty miles away to his used car lot, then headed back for the other seven vehicles.

This had been his best season in thirty years, and the next 2 weekends were booked solid, as were most available dates for the following summer. Business was good and he really loved serving his customers.

Thunder Blood Storm

A sudden, swift wind tore through Big Moose Lake campground in western Maine. Dave King and Glen Swanzy put on their raincoats as they walked out of the ranger's cabin next to the General Store.

"Looks like Hope's closing up early tonight," Dave said at the sight of the front porch lights going off.

"Might as well. This storm's going to be a bad one. I expect everyone is hunkering down to ride her out," Glen said as he opened his door of the Bronco.

Dave got in the passenger side as the first drops of rain tapped against his plastic covered hat. A burst of lightning lit up the empty parking lot and revealed some of the campsites just beyond.

"I hope this doesn't turn into one of those rains like they had in Alstead, New Hampshire. Our weather map looked like a huge amount of rain was coming."

Glen started the Bronco and shifted into drive, then pulled onto the narrow road that wound for over two miles through the wooded campground. It usually took about fifteen minutes to drive the entire road if you kept to the 10 mph speed limit.

"That was a mess. Heard some of the insurance companies still haven't paid up. Guess the whole idea is for them to take your money but never have to pay you any back."

"The whole government's controlled by bankers and corporations. That's why those Vermonters wanted out of the union," Dave said under the glow of the dashboard.

The rain let loose as thunder rolled above them and occasional flashes revealed daylight like glimpses of the campgrounds. The red, yellow, and orange leaves jumped out at them whenever the blackness of the night vanished with a burst of lightning.

"Funny, I wasn't aware Vermont had joined the Union," Glen said.

Dave chuckled, "They probably say the same thing about us. I know we have more flannel shirts per capita than they do."

"My wife's family is from the Grafton area. Nice folks, great pub. They have a general store where people still sit on the front porch and shoot the breeze."

They passed through the small covered bridge that led to the camping area. The boards rattled under their tires and the rain temporarily stopped its drumming on their roof as they entered the bridge. Thrust back into the storm, they passed between the first two rows of campsites.

"A night like this makes me think of that tiny village near Portland where everyone just vanished one October in the 70's," Dave said.

"Always heard it called The Lot. Same thing happened in Dudley Town. I wouldn't set foot in either one, for any amount of money," Glen said.

The lightning flashed twice, lighting up the tree lined road, then complete darkness returned a second later.

"Great, now the power's out," Dave said. "I'll never understand why anyone camps after Labor Day anyway. Too cold and too many bad storms."

"At least it's not real cold tonight. God forbid we go camping without our electric heaters. These people's idea of roughing it is a 27 inch TV," Glen said.

"Look out," Dave said as he pointed at the rain-drenched windshield.

Glen jammed the breaks down hard and they both leaned forward as be barely missed hitting a black Labrador. The dog darted across the road, looked at them, then ran back across the road and laid down in front of a green and white pop up camper.

They both sat silently for a moment, collecting their thoughts amongst the rumbles and drippings of the storm.

"That looked like Rachel Bethel's dog. I'll go see why it's running loose, Dave said.

"That's her usual spot. It has to be her dog, but she never let's that dog off its leash. I think I'll go with you in case something's wrong."

Dave and Glen stepped out of the Bronco and walked over to her camper door. When she did not answer his knocking after several minutes, Dave shot Glen an ominous look. The black lab scratched at the door and whimpered, undaunted by the down pouring rain. "Mrs. Bethel, Mrs. Bethel, are you alright?"

"We'd better go in," Glen said, and opened her camper door as he pulled out his Mag Light. "Are you alright Mrs. Bethel? It's ranger Glen and Dave ma'am." Glen stepped up into the camper, Dave close behind with his flashlight now on and scanning the darkness of her camper.

"Good God," Dave said as his light caught her wide-open mouth, frozen as if in the middle of a scream, lying in the right side bunk. Her dog leapt up to her, smelled her, then whined and fled back out the door into the storm. "Her neck's covered in blood."

Glen spun his light over in the same

direction. He inched closer. "That's not blood as much as it's the muscle in her neck."

"Oh man, you're right. The skin from her neck is gone," Dave said as he covered his mouth with his free hand. "How? Why? This was the first time she went camping since her husband died, and this happens to her on our watch?"

"I know you always liked her, but she's very much dead, very clearly murdered," Glen said. "We'll have to tend to her later."

"We'd better check the other campers first," Dave finished as Mrs. Bethel's roof pinged under the downpour of rain. As they headed back outside, the image of her terrified face gnawed at his consciousness. "Looks like the dog took off. It may be our only witness." They climbed back into the Bronco and began to creep around the campground again.

"I don't suppose your cell phone's working?" Glen asked. As he leaned over the steering wheel, his eyes locked onto the narrow path of light cut by the headlights.

Dave fished it out of his holster and flipped it open. "No, not at all. This rain's killing any chance of a signal."

"Then it's just us, and not much time to warn two hundred campers." Glen stopped the Bronco and turned it off. "Though I know it has the ring of stupidity to it, we'll have to split up."

"You take the left side of the road, I'll

take the right. That way we're never more than thirty feet apart. Make sure we keep an eye on each other's flashlight beam."

"Yell if you see anything suspicious. All we have are our knives," Glen said as he stepped outside of the Bronco into the storm.

"Just tell them there's a prowler. Starting a panic won't help." Dave got out and started knocking on camper doors.

First, he checked two RVs, one tent, a pop-up, then a bus someone had turned into a camper, and everyone seemed fine. He recognized most of the faces, even if only vaguely. He checked after each stop for Glen's light. He saw him walk around a heavily wooded corner, and he could only see a faint glow now, not the actual beam of his light. Better hurry, he told himself. We need to keep in sight of each other. One more motor home to check then he'd run down the road to the next batch of campsites and they would once again be parallel. He'd have to be quick. With them waving lights around, they were an easy target for whatever monster had done that to Mrs. Bethel. Her face burned in his eyes a he rapidly knocked on the next camper.

"Park ranger. We have a prowler. I'm just checking to see if you're O.K. or happened to see anything."

A movement came from inside, then footsteps, as the camper creaked and groaned until the footsteps stopped.

"Who is it?" a man's voice asked.

"Park ranger Dave. Just needed to make sure you're fine. We have a prowler in the campground."

"No prowler here. I keep that door locked, even when we take walks in the afternoon. You can't be too safe."

"Sir, could you open the door so I can verify your identity?"

"Just a minute, let me get my pants on," the voice said. From inside came the sound of more walking, then rustling.

Dave looked over his shoulder in search of Glen's light. He saw a dim glow, but he wasn't even sure if it was from Glen's light or a camper's gas light. "Sir, I'm in quite a hurry. This is an urgent matter."

"I gotcha. I'm almost dressed."

"Sir, please," Dave urged.

"Cool your engines Sonny, there ain't much a prowler's going to nab here anyways except some coolers or some firewood," the man said.

Dave looked back at the wooded corner. He no longer saw the glow. Glen was getting too far ahead of him. He pulled out his radio and called Glen. "I'm lagging buddy, could you hold up? I can't see your light anymore." A screech sounded as he let go of the button to hear Glen's reply, but none came. "Glen, do you read me?" Again, only silence as the rain beat down in steady drops on his raincoat and hat.

Then the camper door swung open in

a sudden burst and smacked Dave. "Sorry about that," the old man said. "Been meaning to fix that, but the wife keeps me too busy to think. She doesn't quite get the notion of what retirement is supposed to mean."

Dave looked him over with a quick glance, then took off, the old man's complaints still rattling on.

"Glen, are you there?" he said into the radio again. Something about the silence felt final. He got to the bend where he had last seen Glen's light and darted his from camper to camper, then across the road. No sight of him anywhere. His chest pounded and his throat tightened while rain dripped down his face. He wondered if anyone who had ever died on the job had feared such an occurrence as they set out for work that day. He ran to the first camper where a man and a woman stood in the opened doorway. "Is everything alright?" the man asked.

"Did another ranger just come by here?"

"Yeah, just a few minutes ago."

"Get in your camper and lock it," Dave said.

"No thief wants to try my door mister," the man said and smiled.

Dave looked at him before leaving and said, "It's more than just a thief." The man's smile vanished.

He knocked on the next one. Yes, he had been there. Then his radio squelched, then a voice, but not Glen's voice, spoke softly.

"Looks like I got another one."

Dave doubted what he thought the barely audible voice had said because of the loud storm. He hurried over to the next camper, where a teen-age girl and her mother verified Glen had also visited their camper. He then sloshed through newly formed puddles and knocked on a small motor home door at campsite 31.

Now he felt terror taking over his body as he waited for someone to answer the door. He shined his light around left, then right, then left again. Then he saw it, under a large Pin Oak tree, in between the campers – Glen's light, partially submerged. He walked over to it and saw the Mag Light rested not in a puddle of rain, but a puddle of blood. He stooped down to pick it up when he heard a man's voice calling from the front of the camper.

He felt watched, stared at, and this feeling made him shine his light up into the tree. The beam hit branches of orange leaves twisting in the wind, then Glen's face appeared, his eyes open, but void of life. His body hung upside down from one of the branches, his feet tied to a limb with his own jacket and most of his throat gone. Dave screamed, then ran to the front of the motor home.

"What's wrong?" the man asked.

Dave struggled to breath or to form

words. He knew the killer maybe watching him, waiting for the right moment to pounce. He hated himself for it, but he felt too terrified to go on.

"Could I come in please?"

"Sure, come in and dry off. My name's Walker." He closed the door behind Dave.

Dave sat down at the table. "Better lock it. There's a killer out there somewhere."

Walker looked at Dave puzzled, then locked the door. "Are you sure about that?"

"Yes. He killed an old lady and now my partner's dead."

Walker sat down at the other side of the table. A small gas lamp hissed in the center of the table and cast a pulsing glow on his face that contained more shadow than light. "That doesn't seem very likely."

Dave looked up at him blankly. "None the less, right now I have to figure out a way to get back to my Bronco with my neck intact so I can go get the sheriff."

"Where's your Bronco?" Walker asked. "Maybe I could go with you. I never met a man who scared me."

Dave watched the door to make sure the handle was not slowly turning. "Then you never met this guy. He likes to tear out people's throats." He looked at Walker for a reaction, but only got a single raised eyebrow. "The Bronco's about one hundred feet behind us if we go straight through the woods, or about three hundred feet or so if we take the road and go back the way we," he paused, recalling Glen's terror filled eyes, "-the way I came."

"Were you the only two rangers here tonight?"

"Except for Hazel, but she's home by now. No one else comes in 'til morning." He listened to the rain hitting the roof and the windshield as the motor home swayed in a sudden wind shear. "I don't suppose another ranger stopped here a few moments ago." A flash of lightning lit up the inside of the camper enough for him to see a black coat hanging on a hook on a door.

"Then it will be several hours before anyone else knows what happened here," Walker said. He stood up as another flash of lightning brushed away the shadows on the walls and floor of the camper.

Something on the floor stirred Dave out of his shock. Why was there a puddle of water under Walker's coat? "You never answered my question. Did my partner stop at your camper tonight?"

Walker paused. "Of course, but don't worry, I'm sure he's hanging around somewhere." He unsnapped the door lock. "Shall we do this? I need to be out of here myself before morning."

"Aren't you afraid?" Dave asked gazing up at the tall man as he reached for his knife in one slow, cautious move.

"I recognize fear, but I don't personally experience it." A thin smile crossed his face. "Why, you're trembling. There's no use to really." He walked past Dave and grabbed the black coat from the hook.

"Why were you out in the storm tonight?" Dave asked as he glanced at the door, now the same distance from both of them.

"I've been here all evening," Walker said, adjusting his coat.

"Then why is there a puddle where your coat had been hanging?"

Walker stopped adjusting. "You are observant, especially for a small town park ranger."

Dave stood stiffly next to the door.

"I'm just passing through, on my way to the lovely little town of Shady Cove." He stepped toward Dave. "But I needed a little snack to tide me over," Walker curled up his upper lip and two long sharp fangs glistened in the gas light.

Dave stared in awe and said as much to himself as to Walker, "But there's no such thing as vampires."

"Belief can not alter reality, neither can disbelief." He buttoned up his coat. "Nor can a piece of forged steel destroy what is eternal."

Dave dropped his useless knife, then jumped up and grabbed the doorknob and twisted, but it didn't budge. I've got to unlock it, he thought. I have to escape this nightmare and get back home to my wife and kids. He unsnapped the lock, twisted the doorknob again and felt the door start to swing open, when an overwhelming force clamped down on his neck and pulled him backwards. He heard the door click shut and a slurping sound.

He clutched at Walker's head, but only for a moment, as his hands fell limp and his legs buckled. Dave felt Walker embracing his body and heard rain slapping the roof while thunder roared. He saw one last flash of lightning as his soul sank into timeless darkness, pursued by the scent of extinguished campfires.

CREEPY'S FAREWELL

If you're reading this, it means you survived my first collection of Creepy Campfire Tales. The next batch will be even more gruesome. Until then you'll have to survive your own horrors lurking just beyond your dimming campfire. But life is like a campfire: The wild, beautiful flames of early evening burn down to brilliant, glowing embers of midnight, which cool toward night's end before turning to ash that is blown away by the start of a new day. Yet the smoke from that fire lingers on forever.

Maybe you'll avoid such creepy terrors if you always look back over your shoulder now and then, just to make sure nothing is there, watching you from the woods or hovering over your campfire.

The hour is late, and your campfire embers are no longer able to repel the darkness or the evil creatures lurking within it, so hurry off to sleep now, before it's too late. After all, my tales are never more than a campfire away.

So if pleasant dreams prove impossible, don't blame me, you're the one who read the book.

But if you do have nightmares, I hope you see something creepy!

CREEPY CAMPFIRE TALES SONG

Creepy Campfire Tales,
Something creepy's going on.
When midnight comes,
The campers scream and run,
Before night's end they'll be dead and gone.

Creepy Campfire Tales,
Something spooky slithers near.
When darkness falls,
Monsters with sharp jaws,
Will arise from The Lake Of Nightmares.

Across foggy waters, a ghost ship sails,
To a haunted forest, Creepy Campfire Tales.
Ghouls and goblins crawl out of graves
Scarecrows dance across hay bales,
Searching for dark campsites,
Creepy Campfire Tales.

When it's hard to believe scary things
you've seen,
Wicked wind blows, & you are in the middle
of Halloween.
When the bony hand on your shoulder is
covered in scales,
And you can't outrun loud ghostly wails,
Your doom will become one of my
Creepy Campfire Tales

OWL CREEK MEDIA LTD

The Source For Seasonal & Holiday Media

1~800~305~0339

Hooty@OwlCreekMedia.com
www.OwlCreekMedia.com

Owl Creek Media Specializes in books, audio, & other media formats that feature stories that take place during a specific season or holiday. Our titles are for ages 5~adult. We also offer Book Fairs, Book Clubs, Reading fund raisers, Author Visits, and the Our Very Own Book Project that publishes books for schools, churches, & other groups to be used as a literacy event, outreach program, inexpensive yearbook, or a fund-raiser.

www.OurVeryOwnBook.com
www.OwlCreekBookFairs.com
www.OwlCreekBookClub.com
www.OwlCreekMedia.com

Visit The Official Web site

www.CreepyCampfireTales.com

For all the latest campground news & horrific updates. Also, Join the official fan club The Camp Fire Club and enjoy exclusive & fun benefits all year long.

To sell these books or other seasonal or holiday titles in your Camp Ground Store, Haunted Attraction, or any other outlet, or for bulk corporate orders, contact Owl Creek Media Ltd for wholesale orders and discounts:
1-800-305-0339

James D. Adams has been involved in the arts his entire life, writing stories, plays, songs, and poems while becoming an award winning musician and actor by 18. He worked as a Morning DJ on WCHI, & co-founded the Kerouc Society poetry group while attending Ohio University. He starred in 4 plays and wrote 2 before writing & starring in "Welcome To Chilli Town" in 1995 at the Majestic Theatre in Chillicothe, Ohio.

He completed consultant & business training through Ohio State University, and worked for 3 years as a trainer & literacy consultant with Scholastic Book Fairs.

He makes dozens of author presentations at schools each year and librarians have called his author visits "lively," "interactive," "entertaining," & "educational."

James now spends his time writing, editing, visiting schools, & teaching creative writing. He lives on 25 acres in Ohio with his wife, Kim & son, Evan.

VISIT THE OFFICAL WEB SITE OF

JAMES D. ADAMS

www.JamesDAdams.com

Enter contests, learn about his latest titles, or book him for an author visit at your school, campground, or haunted attraction.

For the latest on his new Horror Series

Dark Valley Ohio, visit:

www.DarkValleyOhio.com

Creepy Campfire Tales

CPSIA information can be obtained at www.ICGtesting.com
Printed in the USA
BVOW060106110912

299942BV00001B/2/A